JEWEL OF THE THAMES

A Portia Adams Adventure

ANGELA MISRI

For my mother, Sheela, and my sister, Ana,
who believed I was a writer before I did.

Other books in the **Portia Adams Adventures** series:

ACKNOWLEDGMENTS

This book would not have been possible without the support of Fierce Ink Press, the first publishers of my Portia Adams series, and my amazing fans all over the world.

Jewel of the Thames: Casebook 1

Toronto, Winter 1929

L ooking back on it, the last year of my mother's life was, for the most part, unremarkable. Sad, but unremarkable, or so I — at the advanced and wise age of nineteen — believed.

Though normally a stoic and happy woman, my mother had been diagnosed by a rather callous doctor as suffering from a cancer in her breast. He made this diagnosis under duress, having previously turned my poor mother away on three separate occasions with pedantic and, it turned out, useless advice.

She weakened both in body and spirit between these visits, her kind blue eyes weighted down with dark circles and her cheeks and collarbones becoming more visible as her appetite all but disappeared. Before she became ill, she and I stood at exactly the same height, but as she got weaker and weaker she had to use a cane to walk. She only returned to the doctor's office at my urging, armed with whatever evidence and reports that I pressed into her trembling hands.

By the fourth visit to this doctor's office, my mother was almost beyond caring about the origin of her illness. My stepfather, never known for his reliability, had finally given up all pretense of support and had packed his bags for the last time. Though I tried my best to convince my mother that we were better off without him, his desertion drained the last of her strength.

I gripped the papers I had copied from the college library in my left hand and my mother's elbow in my right, and we climbed the two flights of stairs that led to the medical offices. The brightness of the offices belied the seriousness of the activities conducted within, though their well-maintained stone architecture better reflected the traditional viewpoints of the doctors inside their walls.

I finally triumphed in arguing her case with the sedentary old man. He admitted that she had all the signs of a dreaded cancer. My triumph was of course vastly overshadowed by the terrifying prospect of surgery. And eyeing this supposed medical expert, I shuddered to think what his record was in terms of cancer patients.

But in a rare moment of decisiveness (at least since my stepfather's departure), my mother listened to her doctor finally give a name to the disease she had been suffering from for more than a year, and then stood on — I am proud to say — barely shaking legs.

She turned up her nose as he hesitantly offered a surgical solution and instead turned to me, offering her elbow once more. She had agreed to revisit this office, she explained as we walked back down the stairs, purely to vindicate my efforts. The cause of her illness was irrelevant; she had made her peace with her imminent death.

No argument I could make would move her from this decision, and I vacillated between anger and denial as she devoted her remaining months to arranging for my future.

So it was that less than three months later, on a morning in early January in the year 1930, I found myself newly orphaned and standing over my dear mother's grave. The frigid Toronto weather had briefly relented, the ice on the ground crunchy but minimal, and the skies above gray but not adding to the snow on the ground.

My mother had few friends, and I had even fewer, a sad fact made evident by the tiny group gathered around her plot. The priest was economical with his words, and before I knew it, I stood alone over her small gravestone, its only noticeable feature the newness of the simple engraving.

The few flowers that had been placed by it had given in to the coldness of their location, shriveling and curling in response to the cold. One of her few requests had been that she be buried next to her mother, my grandmother, for whom I was named.

Now, looking down at the two nondescript graves, I couldn't help but notice the cracks in the older one, filled in by ice and snow and years of moss, the engraving of my grandmother's name, Constance Adams, showing clearly how many years it had been since she died. Someone had been by to clean out the moss on the two larger headstones to my left and right, and the remains of ribbons could still be seen, the last remnants of bouquets long since gone, making me sorry that no one had cared for my grandmother's grave as well.

I felt the full weight of my loneliness drop over my shoulders like a weighted cowl. My mother was my best friend, my confidante, my only supporter in this whole world, and the loss was magnified a hundredfold by her importance in my life.

Perhaps it was that burden that caused me not to notice a figure steal into the cemetery. Then came the sound of a throat being cleared behind me.

"Oh!" I said, turning toward the stranger in surprise.

In front of me stood a woman of elderly grace, bowed but still haughty of bearing, swathed in furs. Her hair had a dark, silvery sheen, expertly wound up into a chignon and shot with a few streaks of her original black. She was tall, only an inch shorter than me, and her slimness was evident even in the white fur coat she wore. She seemed amused by my startled response, and only my respect for my elders and the setting kept me from glaring at her.

"Yes?" I asked instead, trying to place her in the small cadre of friends my mother had introduced me to over the years.

"You are Constance?" she replied, her accent not wholly American, though with distinct hints of New York in her pronunciation of the word 'are.'

"My middle name is Constance, my first is Portia," I corrected, automatically deciding that her finery meant she could not have run in my mother's far humbler circles.

"Ah, yes." She nodded, stepping closer and pointing her cane at my grandmother's headstone. "Named for your grandmother, obviously."

I tilted my head in acknowledgement, waiting for her to offer the appropriate sympathies so that I might be left to my mourning in peace.

Instead she stepped around me, remarkably agile for a woman of her advanced years, to stand directly in front of my grandmother's grave, parallel to my own position in front of my mother's. The rings on her fingers glinted in spite of the dull light, and the scent of an expensive French perfume I recognized from the waiting room of my mother's doctor's office wafted pleasantly out of her collar, combining with the smell of newly turned earth that had preceded her arrival.

A traveler, I guessed, looking at the variation of fashion she presented, the coat manufactured here in Canada but purchased at least a season ago. She had also recently returned from Europe, if the buckles on her boots were to be trusted. Her gloves were made of an animal skin I did not recognize, leading me to run through a list of countries known to export ladies' fashion.

She ran her eyes over me in a way that made me for the first time in days wonder at my appearance. I never did take much time in front of the mirror, my long dark hair much easier to handle when pulled back in a bun, though invariably a few strands would escape to curl at my forehead and nape.

My mother had tried to convince me of the value of a bit of makeup, but any additional color made me look startling, the blueness of my eyes seeming to blare out of my painted face. That thought made me remember how my mother had often described my eyes as the color of the periwinkle flower, and I had to grit my teeth to stop the tears from starting anew.

My curiosity finally got the better of me when she remained silent in thought through all of this reflection. "I am sorry," I said, breaking the silence, "did you know my mother?"

"Hmm?" she replied, her eyes still on Constance Adams' headstone. "Well, yes, I suppose, when she was young ... but not really. I was a contemporary of your grandmother. We met in Britain and then grew closer when we both lived in San Francisco."

"Ah," I answered, absorbing that, but not really understanding.

I turned my eyes back to my mother's grave for a few seconds of speculation, and then had to ask, "But then what brings you to my mother's funeral today? Are you attending as a friend of my grandmother?"

The older woman gave a most unladylike snort. "Oh, heavens no, I am not that sentimental nor that kind. No, I was contacted by your mother's lawyer, my dear. I am to attend the reading of your mother's will."

We shared a civil yet silent cab ride to the attorney's office — she possibly lost in memories of my grandmother, and I wondering what my sickly, middle-income mother could have left of interest to this obviously wealthy old woman.

I spent my time surreptitiously observing my cab-mate's dress — from her perfect makeup to her impeccable posture to her wrinkled but still beautiful face. She seemed to have a constant smile at her lips, but it was an odd smile, not one of happiness *per se*, more like the smile of someone who knows the answer to a riddle. It was unsettling, to say the least. I had almost managed to form one of the many thoughts in my brain into a coherent question when the cabbie announced our arrival.

Before I could argue, my older companion had paid the fare and I jumped to follow her out onto the street.

I had only met my mother's lawyer on two occasions. The last time he had kindly stopped by our house late in my mother's illness when she was unable to come to him for some required signatures.

After shaking my hand and offering his sympathies, he ushered us into his shabby offices and then reached into his large desk, hunting for the appropriate papers. I tried not to be distracted by an empty birdcage in the corner and took the seat I was offered. The last time I was in this office a noisy budgie had lived here, along with a very friendly orange cat. Neither was present anymore; even the cat hair was missing from the chairs, though still visible on the trouser legs of the lawyer who spoke to us now.

"I am very glad that you both came, ladies. As you are the only two people named in the will, this makes matters very simple," he said, adjusting his shiny glasses on his snub nose.

My companion nodded regally, but I was once again surprised, this time at my stepfather's exclusion from the will, which I expressed aloud.

"Ah, yes," noted the attorney, taking off the precariously balanced glasses and polishing them with a nearby cloth. He would do better to take them straight back to the shop he had purchased them from for an adjustment, but I didn't interrupt. "He too was most shocked not to be mentioned at all in your mother's will, when he found out early this morning."

That he had stopped by the attorney's office instead of attending his wife's funeral was not surprising to a stepdaughter who knew him well, but I couldn't help the quiver of anger I felt on my poor mother's behalf. I glanced away from the lawyer to hide my angry look, directing my gaze at the window for a moment, and noticed a few small brown fingerprints on the sill.

"Yes, he left most unhappy, threatening to return with his own representation and contest the will," the man continued, pulling my attention back toward him. "And all of this without even knowing the contents of the documents."

Before this morning, I would surely have agreed that nothing in my mother's meager belongings was worth a legal battle. But taking a sidelong glance at the finely dressed woman sitting beside me, I was beginning to suspect that all was not as it seemed.

The attorney cleared his throat, unfurling a long sheaf of paper. "This is the last will and testament of Marie Jameson, née Marie Adams," he read in his thin, reedy voice. "I hereby set down that all assets under my name, or wholly belonging to me and no other, shall pass to my only daughter, Portia Constance Jameson."

So far, not surprising. I glanced at the older woman to my left for her reaction, but saw none.

"In addition, I leave all property also to my only daughter, the aforementioned Portia Constance Jameson."

I opened my mouth to ask what assets those might be, but was surprised into silence by an old hand that reached between our two chairs to grasp mine. I looked down at our now joined hands and then back up at the older woman, surprised to see tears in her eyes for the first time since meeting her.

"What property?" I finally managed, wondering if he meant our family home, and not relishing the idea of wresting its ownership away from my stepfather.

The attorney held up his hand, though, and said, "Finally, but with no less weight and responsibility, I leave the care and education of my dearest child, Portia Constance Jameson, to Mrs. Irene Jones of New Jersey — address enclosed."

Looking back on that moment, an outsider would have been hard-pressed to decide who was more shocked at that last piece of information. Mrs. Jones and I looked at each other, and then back at the man sitting across from us.

I had spent the last few months with my mother reiterating again and again that she need not worry about me, that I was old enough to take care of myself. She would smile and nod weakly, but I knew that the worry about what would happen to me was all-consuming for her. It seemed that she had come up with a solution without advising me, and if Mrs. Jones' surprise was genuine, without advising my new guardian either.

"But ... but I don't need a guardian," I blurted out. "I am nineteen years old, sir, and capable of living on my own."

The gentleman smiled gently at me. "You have never had a job, Ms. Jameson, and while it is true that you have reached adulthood, owning property and therefore paying taxes and taking on legal responsibility requires that you be twenty-one years old."

I gaped at him, my brain whirring at this piece of data but unable to refute it since I had never thought about this circumstance.

"That is all, ladies, in terms of the will. There are other papers, of course, that I must share with you." He pulled out an envelope.

"This is the deed to the property in London, left to your grandmother and then to your mother, and now to you, Miss Jameson."

I was still unable to speak, so he continued: "And these are the divorce papers signed by both your parents last week, dissolving their marriage, and removing Mr. Jameson from responsibility to you, his former stepdaughter." He glanced at me. "If you would prefer to change your name back to your birth name in light of this, my dear, we can do that immediately. Your mother suggested that I have the paperwork written up and ready for you, anticipating that you might."

Having been essentially raised by a single mother (after my father was lost in the Great War), I was not pained by the dissolution of my relationship with my former stepfather. Nonetheless, it felt like I was being assailed with life changes at breakneck speed.

Mrs. Jones recovered first. "Surely that is enough. Sir, the poor child has lost her mother and now her stepfather in the same day."

The attorney agreed heartily, and while I sat, weakly absorbing all that had befallen me, they finalized the process whereby I was passed from loving mother to complete stranger with a few signatures. Even with my limited knowledge of the law, I understood that it would not help to beg or argue at this time, so I read the agreements quickly, as was my skill, and then signed where they told me.

The one paper that I found easiest to sign was the one that returned my birth name to me. From now on, I would be known as Portia Constance Adams.

I resolved, as Mrs. Jones pulled on her gloves, to work on this older woman's kindness to maintain my freedom, though where I would go without friends or family, I knew not.

My plan that I had shared with my mother to try to alleviate her stress had been to try to find work in the local library or schools, to earn enough money to continue my education. During my mother's quick decline I had done my best to actually secure such a position, but had so far been unlucky in my interviews.

My social skills were my downfall, and any patience I might have had for speaking to people had been rubbed raw by the worry over my mother's condition. At the best of times I could be impatient, so at my worst I was perceived as rudely dismissive. I knew exactly how much money my mother had left in her bank account and had calculated how much longer I could afford to live without a job. It was not long, and I was too proud to say any of this aloud to either the lawyer or this older woman I had just met.

But now there were new options to consider. Perhaps there were opportunities with this new place in London? I could start a new life there ... free from the loving memories of my mother's presence in my otherwise solitary life.

I shook hands with the attorney, advising him to forgive the cat he had banished from his offices since a child had been the downfall of the bird, not a feline at all. The scratches on the birdcage were months old, while the small, sticky chocolate fingerprints on the cage door were less than a week old.

He looked shocked and glanced wordlessly over at his birdcage, so I walked over to the nearest window to point to the matching chocolate fingerprints where a child had released the budgie into the skies of Toronto. I took the papers and envelopes he held out and then followed my new guardian out the door.

Why had my mother chosen this stranger as my guardian? Was she a distant relation? My grandmother, mother and for a brief time, my father, were the only family I had ever known. I was more intellectually curious than emotionally curious about our extended family, but my grandmother had been adamantly tightlipped about any other relations.

My mother couldn't give me information she didn't have, and she had struggled for decades with her own mother's stubborn reticence. In her last months of life, my mother had admitted, her eyes dropping from mine in that conversation as I now recalled, that her own research had failed to turn up anyone suitable.

Now, as Mrs. Jones hailed a cab, I looked carefully at her features, the distinct profile of her nose and chin, and saw nothing that resembled my mother's or my grandmother's features. She seemed to have known my grandmother — was she somehow indebted to our family through that relationship?

I automatically sat down in the cab as Mrs. Jones waved me in encouragingly.

"You certainly surprised the man with your observations about his poor bird, didn't you?" she remarked, adjusting her gloves.

"Probably the average reaction. I must assume that your mother said nothing to you of this arrangement?"

I shook my head, tears of anger starting now as I contemplated this betrayal by my closest and dearest relative. Why keep this from me? Did she think me so uncooperative?

To be fair to her, I knew that if she had shared this with me I would have vehemently fought the plan — I was a solitary person, and the idea of being under the guardianship of anyone other than my own mother was abhorrent. I sniffed, realizing that my mother had been right to approach this plan without telling me. Not that it made the current situation any better.

"Oh, now, don't work yourself into a state," Mrs. Jones admonished, pulling a monogrammed hanky out of her large purse and handing it to me. "She had her reasons, I am sure. And I am most flattered that she would give me such a responsibility. I had not considered that she would."

I couldn't bring myself to agree. The whole situation was just too new. I shook my head at my immature reaction. I should have planned for this! I could have! And then maybe my mother wouldn't have left me with — I glanced at Mrs. Jones from beneath tear-laden lashes — this woman.

I had no desire to live with a stranger, but I didn't have the financial ability to strike out on my own. Our home in Toronto was heavily mortgaged, I knew, and a home in London in my name was all well and good — but how to get there? And what to do when I arrived? Perhaps I could sell the property from here, take the money and invest that in my future.

As I was folding and unfolding the hanky, monogrammed with an I, an A, and an H in flowing script, the cab came to a stop. I recognized my family home. Only two days ago my mother's body was being carried out on a stretcher to the hearse that would bear her out of my life forever. I swallowed painfully, shutting my eyes against that memory and forcing myself to think of all the other moments we had spent here.

Opening my eyes determinedly, I had to admit I was also embarrassed for this fine lady to see where I lived. The brick house was tiny, with a front porch that leaned to the right, its posts having been bolstered with cheap beams in lieu of actually fixing the underlying issues with the structure.

 The exterior had never been painted, at least in my memory, and the once-wooden trim showed this fact the most, made all the more obvious by the shiny cleanliness of the windows, on which my mother had focused her diminishing energy despite my arguments. I stepped out of the cab, my eyes on the front door, listening to Mrs. Jones tell the driver to wait for us.

My eyes were thus fixed because across the doorway was a chain and a lock, barring entrance to the house. As I strode forward, I spied my former stepfather leaning against the rusted chain-link fence, smoking a thin cigarillo. I stopped abruptly as he recognized me and hauled his flabby frame straight.

"Ya finally showed up, did ya?" he slurred at me, obviously deep into his cups despite the hour. I ignored his tone, instead pointing to the door. The smell of his preferred cheap whiskey assaulted me as I ran my eyes over his clothes, trying to assess just how long he had been drinking. His boots were relatively dry, indicating that he had at least changed since last night, perhaps to attend the lawyer's office. But the grungy neckerchief showcased his last three meals at least, his graying chest hair appearing above the stained white cloth. I calculated his last shave was at least a week ago, and I shook off my disgust with effort to ask:

"What has happened? When I left this morning—"

"They came after you left, the gits," he interrupted, pulling a crumpled-up piece of paper out of his pocket and handing it to me as my new guardian stepped closer.

Dreading the note, and yet strangely already anticipating its contents, I quickly scanned it. The basic message was unsurprising: his creditors had seen my mother's death as the final sign they would never get their money back (a fact I agreed with since my mother was the only person in our household who contributed to the mortgage) and had seized the house as soon as her death was officially announced.

Mrs. Jones and my former stepfather were eyeing each other with what looked like equal disdain, so I dumbly handed her the note and made to look at the door more closely. The lock was secure, so I chose the simpler route, edging around the side of the house to the east window we had never gotten around to mending. Pulling it up, I easily entered my former home, wasting no time on the overturned furniture or broken fripperies. I guessed the state of the house was from the creditors hurriedly seeking out any valuables, but it could have just as easily been my former stepfather doing the same.

I made straight for my mother's room, and taking a worn traveling bag from her closet, scooped a few photographs and memorabilia into it.

From her bedside table I picked up the precious photo of her wedding day, running my finger over my father's visage.

Looking around the room at the quiet femininity of the homemade lace pillow covers and the soft pink of the crocheted blanket, I sat down heavily on her neatly made bed. My mother would have been mortified at the condition of her house, having worked so hard to keep it clean and sparkling despite her ex-husband's and (I had to admit) my own more slovenly lifestyle.

 It was only in the past few months, when she had to rely on me in her weakness, that it had fallen far below her standards, cobwebs apparent in the corners of the room and the wooden floors lacking their usual shine. And now with the contents of the house in disarray,

I purposely turned my eyes toward her personal effects. Her medicines were still laid out on the vanity. Her journal was still tucked under her pillow. If I closed my eyes, I could still smell that curious mix of lemon and cinnamon that had followed my mother around in her final months. What was I going to do? This house was not even mine anymore. I was out of time, dramatically so.

Scrubbing at my wet cheeks with my knuckles, I dug into my purse to pull out the few bills I had left, counting them out. Probably enough for one night at a hotel, but not much more. I shoved them into the traveling bag, adding the wedding photo and my mother's journal.

I leaned down under the bed to pull out my mother's jewelry box, not surprised to find that it had been raided, probably by my former stepfather. I clutched at my mother's silver cross around my neck. The funeral director had handed it back to me by this morning before the burial, and really that was the only piece I would have missed. The cross was tiny, half the length of my pinkie, handed down from my grandmother at her death, and now to me. The chain was slim but dropped the cross itself right at the base of my collarbone, resting there coldly but comfortably, as if it had always been so. I shuddered at the thought that my stepfather might have denied me even this tiny memory of my mother.

I slammed the lid of the jewelry box shut and threw it back under the bed, feeling the urge to scream out loud but somehow stifling it and instead leaping to my feet to stalk to my own room.

I was in no way a clotheshorse, so I saved room for some favorite books, a well-worn pair of walking shoes and a traveling coat. I looked around, remembering better times, and had to again fight the urge to scream. The hours I had spent as a child, waiting for her to get home from one of her many jobs, cuddled on her bed wrapped in her oldest shawl and reading whatever newspaper or journal she had brought home from the library for me. How she would carry me from this bed to my own when I fell asleep waiting, and gently kissed my head before pulling the covers up over me. I couldn't be here any longer. What had made me think I could be here after my mother was gone?

Hearing a raised voice outside, I quickly climbed back out the way I had come.

I was shocked to see my former stepfather shouting at Mrs. Jones, inches from her face. She was silent in her disgust as he accused her of stealing from him and demanded recompense for whatever my mother's will had promised her.

My anger was well stoked by the time I reached her side, as much on behalf of my poor mother as my new guardian, neither of whom deserved this man's bile.

She said not a word to him but extended her hand to me, which I readily took, and, while the neighbors gathered to see what the fuss was about, we headed toward our waiting cab with as much dignity as we could. My former stepfather made the further mistake of reaching out to grab at my shoulder as we had almost gained the sidewalk, and that was when the last astonishing thing happened on that horrible day full of surprises.

Mrs. Jones turned and planted her cane between his legs near the ankles so that his momentum caused him to trip and fall in a cursing heap on the ground behind us. Instead of bolting for the cab, as I thought she would, she stood over him that way, her cold eyes daring him to stand and confront us again. He was a coward to his very soul, though, and gritting his teeth, he just crawled away, hobbling on his injured ankle and grumbling under his breath.

The last of my ties to this city had been cut; this house was no longer my home, the pathetic man crawling away was no longer my stepfather and I was ready to leave all of this behind. I looked expectantly at Mrs. Jones, wondering if it would be difficult to persuade her to let me move to London, a city I had always longed to visit but never dreamed of traveling to. A city that was as far away from my crushing memories as possible.

"All done, then, m'dear?" she enquired, turning to me.

"Indeed," I answered with finality, turning my back on the only home I had ever known.

CHAPTER TWO

W HAT AN odious man," Mrs. Jones declared almost as soon as we turned the corner, her hazel eyes flashing with anger. "I will never understand why your mother married that beast."

I shrugged, remembering all the arguments my mother and I had over him and resolving never to think of him again. "He was a waste of my mother's time, and I warrant would be a waste of yours should you spend any thought on his existence, ma'am."

She looked surprised at my bile, but approving, and her mouth slowly quirked up, the pink lipstick she wore a perfect shade for her skin color.

"Well, at least that makes your decision a little easier, Portia Adams," she prompted, reaching into her purse to pull out a small hand mirror and adjusting her hair, which had not moved at all as far I could tell.

"My decision, ma'am?" I asked, suddenly wondering where the cab was taking us. "I don't understand."

"You will come with me to London, as soon as it can be arranged," she answered, her eyes still on her mirror as she smiled, checking her teeth, and finding all as it should be, snapping the silver compact closed.

I looked down at my hands, nodding slowly. "There is nothing for me here, it is true, but ... London? I've never been there. I know no one there."

She tilted her head. "Who is it you know here?"

I flushed, aware of my solitude and for the first time in my life embarrassed by it.

"And you know me now," she continued, placing her gloved hand on my knee and leaning toward me. "I know you don't really need a guardian. Anyone with two eyes and a brain can see you are a most capable woman. But I can help you. Think of me as more of a benefactor than a guardian — someone who has interest in your success."

My lack of skill in social niceties also meant that I had trouble trusting new people, but looking at this regal old woman, I felt no animosity emanating from her. Also, my mother had obviously trusted her enough to leave me in her care, even if I did not need it.

"So ... London," I said, sitting back, my eyes still on this stranger, running through her possible motivations: indebtedness to my family? Interest in this house in London?

"London," she agreed with a sigh as she sat back.

We spent the night at a hotel, paid for by my new guardian despite my objections. I knew that I had no right to be so proud; I had so little money to spend that any help she could offer should be accepted with thanks and grace.

At some point that first evening over an extravagant supper in our rooms, I managed to express my thanks. In the depths of my grief and then shock, it struck me that I had yet to do that. The meal consisted of warm beef stew and two kinds of buttered breads along with salads, cheeses and fruits. I took my cue from Mrs. Jones. Rarely had such an array been laid out before me, and I copied the order of foods she chose and the different cutlery she used to ingest them.

She smiled, recognizing my watchful mimicry before saying, "I owe your mother far more than money or support, and I owe your grandmother more than I could ever repay for her friendship when I most needed it. We need not speak of this again, but know I can not only comfortably afford to be your guardian, but it is my honor and pleasure to repay your family in this way for all they have given me."

"I have to ask, what is it that you owe my mother?" I said. "And surely the friendship of my grandmother was paid in full by your friendship in return?"

Mrs. Jones shook her head adamantly. "No, you can't possibly understand the significance of your grandmother in my life. And even were it not so, my respect for the woman demands that I do everything I can to make sure her granddaughter is well-established and happy."

Aside from more expressions of thanks for the friendship she had enjoyed with the first Constance Adams, I could get nothing further from Mrs. Jones. I must admit that I was overwhelmed by this amount of social interaction and was thankful for the longer periods of silence I was granted over the next few days to come to terms with my new circumstances.

The first night I woke sweaty and soaked in tears, clutching my pillow like a vise, and it took several hours to fall back asleep. In the morning I woke late to the sound of a person brushing her teeth in the bathroom, and I painfully swallowed down the knowledge that it could not be my mother. She was dead. How strange to me.

Whatever her motivations, Mrs. Jones had a strange insight into what other people in my life — teachers, friends of my mother — had called my 'moods'. At first I thought she shared my solitary predilections, but watching her interact with staff at the hotel and the various socialites who would stop by our table when we were eating and taking note of her daily routine, I decided that wasn't it at all.

"I don't really like being around crowds of people," I blurted out one afternoon as we bought tickets for our train trip down to New York, where we would board an ocean liner to take us the rest of the way to England.

My guardian looked at me quizzically with the small smile I was becoming accustomed to. "Why, yes dear, I know."

"And I like time to think. Every day. In quiet reflection," I continued, watching her reaction, which was minimal except to nod slowly, the smile still in place.

It was my turn to look quizzical. "But how is it you know? Was my grandmother the same? If so, my mother never mentioned it to me."

To my surprise, that question elicited a chuckle from the older lady, who deftly scooped up our tickets and tucked them into her fashionable purse before turning my way and taking my elbow. "Lord no, your grandmother was a terror on the social scene. She had a laugh you could hear from four tables over, and loved balls and parties more than anything else in life. She would plan for them for months, and I would have to drag her out of those events at all hours of the morning!"

I shook my head, never having known these details, but believing nonetheless in the picture Mrs. Jones painted of my namesake. It was in these brief moments when curiosity overtook despair that I allowed myself to think of my future rather than dwell in my present.

I took to reading a page in my mother's journal in the evenings, running my hands over the handwriting, trying to smile through my tears at the memories she had preserved here. Most of the journal was about me. That in itself made me cry because I really had felt like the center of her world, and she obviously agreed. Each entry was only about a paragraph and described anecdotes of daily activities that she found amusing or worrying or just wanted to remember.

My first steps were described (skinned my knees because I was determined to have my first walk on gravel). The pride was evident in her account of my being promoted from grade one to three, though her next entry was a worried one centered on my lack of friends. She was right in that I had very few friends in school, but wrong to take on the guilt that her allowing me to move up a grade early was the cause. I was the cause. I was far more interested in education than the children around me.

My prospects in Toronto had been limited by circumstance, having reached the pinnacle of academic success against all odds, much to the embarrassment of my former stepfather. He took great pleasure in reminding me that my schooling was to come to an undramatic end on my twentieth birthday, when he intended to marry me off. How my mother had afforded tutors and lessons for almost two decades I had never known, but I took to learning with the zeal of a long-serving inmate finally granted his freedom.

We had booked an overnight compartment for our train trip south, so I watched the sun set over Toronto as we pulled out of the station, saying a silent goodbye to my home of so many years. My companion quickly fell asleep with her book lying over her chest, so I closed it and pulled a small blanket out of the overhead cabinet to cover her with. It took me a few hours to fall asleep. Even the rocking motion of the train did not soothe my churning brain. So it was, as we pulled up into the station in New York, that I raised with my new guardian the subject of continuing education.

"Well, it just so happens that I have written ahead to a friend, well, let's call her a friend for now ... and applied for your admission to King's College," she offered, a sparkle in her eye.
"That is most kind of you, Mrs. Jones," I answered, my heart beating wildly at the opportunity, "but surely the tuition—"

"The cost is not your concern, my dear. I can afford it," she interrupted. "Does studying at the college appeal to you?"

"Very much so," I replied, shaking off the guilt as best I could, and only partially succeeding. My brain seemed to want to linger on the life I had enjoyed with my mother, and my heart seemed to want me to feel bad for anything else.

Mrs. Jones broached the subject quite unprompted the morning after arriving in New York, in the downstairs lobby of the hotel, asking what my mother's plans had been for me.

"For if I am to stand in as your guardian, I should know what your mother wanted for you," she explained.

I looked down at the scone that had until moments ago smelled heavenly of blueberries and butter. Now it might as well have been a finely formed rock; that's how my appetite changed at the mere mention of my past life.

"She worked so hard to make sure I had the best education, that I wanted for nothing," I started to say, my eyes still on my plate, "I..."

"You miss her," Mrs. Jones finished, reaching across the table to cover my hand. I nodded, not looking up.

"You will miss her," she continued. "You will miss her every single day for a long time."

The melancholy in her voice made me raise my eyes to meet hers, the trembling of her lower lip underscoring just how deeply she sympathized with my situation. I guessed that she had lost someone important to her, perhaps recently, and I was grateful for her experience.

"And then you'll miss her a tiny bit less, and a tiny bit less," she continued, tilting her head to the side as she spoke, the low tremor in her voice still apparent, "but if you think you are doing her memory justice by feeling guilty about pursuing a path she would have chosen..." Mrs. Jones shrugged daintily, allowing me to finish the logical argument she had made without any words at all.

"Who did you lose?" I asked, swallowing down the lump in my throat.

She jerked away from me at the question, her eyes on her lap as she struggled to regain her composure.

"I can only assume that your advice comes from experience," I explained, watching her take a deep breath.

"Yes, well, my dear girl, when you get to my advanced age," she answered finally, carefully taking up her teacup, "a great many of your friends and family will have passed. And it is sad every single time."

I still believed her to be talking about a specific loss, but in a moment of sensitivity that I usually ignored, I let it pass.

Our conversations on that long trip grew when we boarded the ocean liner that would take us across the Atlantic. I had never traveled by ship before and was understandably excited by every aspect of this new adventure. Mrs. Jones had booked us into first-class suites along the outside of the ship, so that my small porthole looked out over beautiful views no matter what time of day. Not that

I spent much time in my suite, preferring to walk the decks and explore everything from bow to stern. Waiters followed first-class passengers everywhere, an aspect of the journey my guardian enjoyed more than I. I became quite impatient with being continually asked about my comfort but found that if I explored below decks, in the second- and third-class areas of the ship, I was left to my own devices. I also had to admit (if only to myself) that I felt more comfortable amongst these folks, with their simple chipped teacups and sandwich-dominated meals, than at the extravagance of the buffet table in the first class dining room.

I discovered early on that Mrs. Jones had a remarkable singing voice, which she carefully managed, not over-stressing it and gargling every night with salt water. She had spent some time on stage, that much was clear from her regal bearing, the way she projected her voice and even the professional way she applied her makeup.

The details of her relationship with my grandmother were still rather unexplained, a situation that annoyed me to no end, though I did manage to glean a most interesting fact: she had also known my grandfather! He was a source of great mystery in my family, especially to my late mother, who had grown up without him. The circumstances of my mother's birth were, it seemed, a closely guarded secret — so much so that my grandmother had refused to speak of them, saying only that "he" was gone.

When my own father died in the war, my mother confessed that she had expected my grandmother to finally share her own loss of a husband, if only to comfort her daughter. But she was wrong; no clarity was ever given to my poor mother as to her filial heritage.

"But then you knew my grandfather, really?" I repeated to Mrs. Jones as the sea pitched beneath us.

"Oh, heavens, yes, I knew your grandfather," she chuckled, puffing on a tiny clay pipe, an affectation that seemed wholly out of place in so dignified and feminine a person.

"What was he like?" I demanded, rapt with attention despite my uneasy belly.

"Like?" she repeated thoughtfully. "He was, well, John was just so remarkably kind and human. Without ego or avarice, sympathetic and caring..."

I nodded, forming in my mind's eye this paragon of a man.

She leaned back, closing her eyes and blowing out a thin wisp of smoke. "He was always a good-looking man. Your eyes are from him, the same blue, but you are slimmer of build and have your grandmother's exotic face rather than his rounder, friendly one. He was a bit of a bounder, as men of his looks are apt to be."

I grinned at this, adding to my mental picture.

"He married as often as..." she blinked, laughed, "well, as often as I did, I suppose, though my reasons were infinitely better."

She glanced keenly at me. "Your grandmother was the first and best of his wives, and he would have been a far happier man had he come to this side of the pond with her rather than returning to England and marrying Mary."

That was all I could persuade her to say that night, and indeed I despaired of gaining any further insights into my grandparents until almost four days later. I was mournfully ill, bent at the waist over my basin, weak and sweaty from seasickness. The voyage to this point had been relatively calm, but as of this morning the skies had darkened, and the seas all around had become choppy and violent. I had missed two meals that I would have normally enjoyed above deck, but was too ill to even pass word to Mrs. Jones excusing myself.

She arrived as I had just managed to regain my bunk, dragging the basin with me onto my stomach as I lay back.

"Oh, my dear, you should have sent for me," she said as she took in the pathetic scene.

I mumbled something barely intelligible about being too weak, but she ignored me, sweeping in, soaking a wet cloth and pressing it over my closed eyes.

I sighed at the relief that brought and took her ministrations with gratitude. So much was I relaxing that I nearly missed her whisper, "Both your grandparents suffered the same seasickness, I remember."

My eyes flew open as I tried to sit up. "They did?"

"Lie back down, you silly girl," she commanded, easily pressing me back into a prone position because of my weakened state.

"But—" I protested.

"If you lie still and try and regain your spirit, I promise I will answer your questions," she said.

I nodded a little too eagerly, bringing on a new wave of nausea. I shut my eyes, willing the sea to cooperate. Meanwhile, she re-soaked the cloth and applied it to my brow.

"As I recall, your grandfather never traveled by sea without a tincture of ground mint to add to cool water," she explained.

"Mint?" I said, taking care not to move.

"A self-prescribed antidote. Do you want me to ring for some from the galley?"

I did, and said so, my reason being as much to relieve my present state as to feel just a little closer to my mysterious grandfather. We sat in rocking silence until the attendant arrived with some fresh mint leaves.

I watched Mrs. Jones crush a few leaves into the jug of water, the pungent smell filling the cabin, and then she soaked the cloth before applying it to my forehead. Whether it was actually a cure or just a placebo of faith in a lost relative, I do not know. I know only that I awoke the next day feeling better than I had in two weeks.

CHAPTER THREE

I expected that we would go straight to Mrs. Jones's home in London (I had learned that she had residences all over the world), but instead she directed the cabbie at the train station to my inherited property.

I peppered her with questions about every landmark we passed: the gothic look of Tower Bridge, the imposing structure of Big Ben, the crimson-dressed guards in front of Buckingham Palace, Lord Nelson's statue in the middle of Trafalgar Square. Everything fascinated me, and she had a story to tell about each.

"Those bronze lions were remarkable when they were put in place under Nelson," she whispered, pointing at the regal feline statues as we passed. "It is one of my fondest memories as a child, when my father brought me to their installation. Though by then Sir Edwin was quite mad, at least according to the gossip at the time."

The traffic in Whitehall took my breath away with the mix of horse carriages, trucks, cars, bicycles and pedestrians all vying for the lane that would allow for the quickest route through the heart of the city.

In between my barrage of questions, Mrs. Jones sang to herself under her breath and her eyes grew moist as we passed through the city.
I was not above my own sense of wonder at finally arriving at my new home, taking in the differences and similarities between

Toronto and bustling London. The age of the city struck me again and again, in its architecture and condition.

It was at once more beautiful and more mysterious than any other city I had been in before, not that I had traveled much at all — once to Montreal, twice to Ottawa in the past ten years and those few days in New York with Mrs. Jones. New shiny awnings fought for my attention with crumbling façades, and every darkened alley seemed to be positively alive with hidden movement.

The sheer number of people on the streets amazed me, and the varieties of dress as well as the different shades of skin were all new. Toronto had its share of immigrants, and a fair number of native Canadian people as well, but they were very much in the minority, especially in the downtown core of the city. I had been introduced to more than a few immigrant groups through my mother's myriad of professions — from house cleaner to nanny to librarian — but in limited circumstances, and never socially. Here people of all races, colors and classes mixed and mingled, bustling through the streets in an equal hurry toward their respective destinations.

I wished that my mother were alive to see it, and I had to blink away a tear remembering her kind face and soft voice. She loved to travel but finances had restricted her ambitions, especially after my father's death.

Their move from San Francisco to Toronto when I was a toddler had been made out of necessity as they sought more job opportunities and lower rents. But she would bring home brochure after brochure from the local travel agency as a way to feed that hunger for new cities and new cultures. I had never really shared that ambition myself, preferring places I knew to places I did not, but no one could be unmoved by my mother's enthusiasm, not even me.

It had been a few weeks since her death, but I still felt her absence sharply and wished for the hundredth time that she were still at my side. Not that Mrs. Jones was failing in her new role as my guardian... I looked over at the older woman. On the contrary, in some ways she and I got along better than my mother and I had. But she would never be able to fill that place in my heart for the only person who had loved me above all others. And whom I had loved the same way.

It took almost an hour for us to wend our way to our destination, and upon arrival, both Mrs. Jones and I leaned out of the cab in excitement.

Before us stood a brick townhouse in reasonable condition, two floors at least with very serviceable steps leading to a nondescript dark green door. The semi-circular stained glass window above the front door displayed the number in black, and a light could be seen within. On the left, or west side of the townhouse, stood an ancient-looking bakery, Greek if I had to guess by the writing on the sign and the smells wafting from it. To the east were another seven townhouses obviously designed by the same hand, and having the same framing, stained glass and style of door.

"If'n you ladies are lookin' for help, you might be better off with the boys at the Yard these days," the cabbie remarked as we made no move to disembark.

I thought that a strange comment, and said so, but he just shrugged and said, "Mr. Holmes hasn't been seen here nigh on fifteen years, I'd say, if not more. But it's your lot, I said m'piece."

Mrs. Jones had by now extended the correct fare to the man and was exiting the cab, so I did the same. As the cabbie pulled away, I turned to Mrs. Jones. "What did he mean — Mr. Holmes?" I asked, looking at the door and feeling my memory claw at me. "Surely he did not mean Sherlock Holmes, the detective?"

Mrs. Jones had meanwhile picked up the doorknocker and given it a sharp rap. "None other, my dear," she answered.

"But why?" I said, stepping back from the front door to look at the full façade of the townhouse. "How did he come to live in the building?"

The door swung open to reveal a good-looking gentleman only a few years my senior, with a half-eaten red apple in one hand. He was almost six feet tall, with wide shoulders, an athletic build and dark brown hair that curled at the forehead over inquisitive brown eyes. For the first time in almost a month I wondered how I looked and reached up to pat down what I was sure were unruly curls trying to escape my hat.

"Afternoon, ladies, what can I do for you?" he asked in a cordial bass voice. His trousers were half of a uniform, though I couldn't place them right away. I glanced at his sleeves and decided against kitchen worker, and then at his hands, deciding against maître d'. Finally my eyes lit on the small loop on his belt revealing the uniform's requirement to carry a baton.

"This is Miss Portia Adams," offered my companion, "and I am Mrs. Irene Jones."

"Ah yes, Mrs. Jones, your letter arrived two weeks ago," he replied, his smile revealing a pair of dimples as he took a bite of his apple and stood aside to allow us entrance into a narrow hallway. "My parents have been expecting you."

I closed the door behind us as the young man was taking my guardian's coat. He took mine with another dimpled smile, and then beckoned us to follow him through a door and into the large sitting room on the main floor.

There sat two middle-aged persons with three middle-aged dogs sitting between them, all in various states of dozing. The sofas and chairs were all covered with a loud floral fabric that had only slightly dimmed over the years, their wooden legs a mix of styles that told a simple story of frugality I recognized from my own mother's furnishing habits.

"Excuse me, they are quite hard of hearing," the man said apologetically, and then taking a deep breath said in a much louder voice, "Mother, Father, our new landlady has arrived."

I blushed at this characterization, having never owned anything to this point, let alone land with tenants. I glanced at the wallpaper in the room, which was as loud as the furniture, with large circular stamps in shades of gray and blue.

The mother jerked awake with a start, turning sleepy eyes on us, but the older gentleman slept right on through, as did the three dogs. I didn't recognize the breed of the dogs, though they all seemed to have a bit of bulldog in them from this angle — at least from their size and the amount of saliva barely held within their jowls. The young man leaned in now to speak directly in his mother's ear.

"Miss Portia Adams, daughter to Marie Jameson is here, remember? She has taken ownership of the house."

This was enough to spark a memory in the woman, and she kindly asked us to sit down and take our ease with a cup of tea.

"We were of course told of your mother's untimely death, my dear," said the woman, who had introduced herself as Mrs. Dawes, reaching out to pat my knee. "How terrible for you, poor thing!"

I thanked her for her solicitude, and she continued. "Your mum was a fine mistress. Raised the rent lightly, left management of the house to myself and now to my son. And we have been good tenants, if I do say so m'self."

I had no idea if they had been, having never heard of this property before the day of my mother's funeral. Mrs. Jones spoke up at this point. "And the upstairs tenant?"

"Oh, moved out months ago. Brian here was takin' advantage of the pause between tenants to fix it up a bit," the woman said, nodding toward her son, who stood behind her chair finishing his apple.

"We were about to put an advertisement in the paper to rent it when the lawyer's letter arrived."

"Ah, perfect! Then Miss Adams will be moving in upstairs as soon as possible," Mrs. Jones said approvingly.

Once again my guardian had made a hairpin turn. I could scarcely mask my surprise. Everyone else in the room, at least those who were conscious, seemed equally surprised.

"Really?" Mrs. Dawes said, looking at us. "The two of you?"

"Oh heavens, no, I travel far too much to be considered an occupant of any one home," Mrs. Jones answered haughtily, dipping her biscuit in her tea. "I will of course drop in from time to time to check on my charge, but I would like to enlist your help in ensuring her safety and care, madam."

Mrs. Dawes sat up straighter at this responsibility and agreed to be of whatever help she could. They arranged a short-term plan wherein I would eat some of my meals with the Dawes as I became accustomed to a new city, but my guardian made it clear that attendance was not mandatory, and was entirely up to me.

There was nothing left to do but to show me to my rooms. I followed Mrs. Dawes up the stairs to a second landing, where she opened the door to a medium-sized sitting room with a lovely brick fireplace. The wallpaper was thankfully muted, a pale gold background with brown fleur-de-lis accents, and the comfortable furniture also seemed to match the mood of the room, in various shades of brown. The wooden floors looked polished and well maintained, and the tiny kitchen was of a reasonable size for a single person.

Everything seemed to be in a decent state, though a little old-fashioned and decidedly male when compared to my mother's sitting room back in Toronto. No doilies or throw pillows, no small pieces of cross-stitch over the backs of chairs. But it was very clean, even the fireplace showing minimal soot, making me wonder if the chimney had been sealed up and the bricks were now a façade rather than a working fireplace.

I will admit to feeling not a little hurt and cross at the seeming ease with which my guardian had passed me off. This was an odd reaction since I enjoyed being in charge of my own life, which living by myself would grant me. But I forgot all about that when I saw the bookshelves in the sitting room.

There were five of these massive dark wooden bookshelves, filled with volumes and reaching from floor to ceiling, their dominance of the north wall interrupted only by the curtains of the two windows.

A glutton for the printed word, I gasped at the treasure before me, barely hearing Mrs. Dawes as she led Mrs. Jones to the bedroom and directed Brian to deliver my meager belongings up here.

I don't know how long I stood there. At some point Brian said from over my shoulder, "I thought it best to bring these back out of storage. You should be the one to decide where they go."

"I should?" I answered, my eyes still locked on the precious tomes, though I could feel how close Brian was, and my stomach fluttered at it.

"Why, yes," he said. "They passed to you the same as this house. And not a few of them were in fact written by your grandfather himself."

I finally tore my gaze from the spines of the books. "My grandfather? These are his books?"

Nodding, he selected a brown journal from the bookshelf and handed it to me. "See?"

I read the cover page — *The Adventures of Mr. Sherlock Holmes, June-August 1882* — and my eyes traveled down to the author's signature: "As faithfully recorded by Dr. John H. Watson."

"Dr. John Watson," I murmured, connecting the dots with a certainty that at once elated and shocked me.

"Your grandfather," corrected Brian with another friendly smile, and he wandered away to speak to his mother.

My mind was humming now, grasping at any story I could remember about the world-famous detective and his trusty sidekick Dr. Watson — my own grandfather! How could this be? How could I have never known this? I pressed a hand to my forehead, thinking back to the few times my grandmother had been coaxed into speaking of her life here in London. I shook my head. No, there had been no clues to lead me to this startling place, no unfollowed leads. It was just a secret my grandmother had been determined to keep.

Mrs. Jones returned to my side, the Dawes having left us on our own. She stood beside me, quietly surveying the books, running her manicured hand lightly over the spines.

"He did love to write down every little exploit." Her fingers paused on one book, and then continued their journey. "Holmes didn't give the good doctor credit for it while he was alive, but I know he appreciated all the attention."

I sat down on one of the comfortable wing chairs. "My grandfather was Dr. Watson, the famous partner to the even-more-famous Sherlock Holmes? My grandmother never told anyone! My mother had no idea..."

"Yes, little one," Mrs. Jones said kindly, but with a slightly sardonic smile. "Your grandparents were married barely a year, just enough time for your mother to be born before they divorced, he staying in England, your grandmother emigrating to the States. Your grandfather remarried several times after that, and he bought 221 Baker Street when the old landlord, Mrs. Hudson, died, at which point I believe the Dawes family moved in."

"And it passed to my mother?"

"Two years ago, when John died," she answered. "His other children have their own estates, two of them being doctors, the other being rather a useless sort, so your grandfather must have thought to leave something to his first child. According to Mrs. Dawes, they never met, corresponding only by letter, and your mother's instructions were to continue running the townhouse as her father did. She wanted as little to do with the place as possible."

I nodded, understanding at once why this inheritance had been left unspoken — to hide it from my selfish former stepfather.

"But then, when John Watson died, and my mother inherited this place, she finally knew who her father was!" I said, the truth obvious now. "She never told me," I added, tears threatening anew, this time from hurt. I looked down at the book in my hands. "Why didn't she tell me?"

Mrs. Jones, her eyes sympathetic and soft, gave a tiny shrug before saying, "I don't know, Portia; as I have told you, your mother and I had not spoken in almost twenty years."

"Fine," I declared, getting angry now, "then why did you not tell me about this, Mrs. Jones? You knew the truth — why not tell me right away?" I pushed the book back into its place on the shelf.

She hesitated, but then said, "Honestly, I wasn't trying to hide him from you, I just didn't know what you knew. And then when you shared with me that your grandmother had adamantly kept all information about John from you, I thought it best to get to know you better. Tell me, if I had told you John's full name the first time we talked about him, what would you have thought? Would you have known he was the same John Watson?"

I shook my head. "Possibly not, but his name, in addition to inheriting 221 Baker Street, would certainly have been enough, Mrs. Jones. You should have trusted me with the full information."

"I see that now, my dear, and I do apologize. I just want you to be introduced to your London connections gently," she said, grasping my hands. "I don't want you to have the reaction your grandmother did, cutting herself off from everyone in this city."

"I barely knew my father, he was taken from us so young. He was an orphan," I explained, my eyes still pointed downwards. "I deserve the truth about my own family.

"No more lies, Mrs. Jones," I declared, getting myself back under control as I turned back toward the bookshelves, pulling out a medical textbook. "No one needs to be careful around me anymore. Just give me all the data, and I promise you, I will deal with it."

Mrs. Jones seemed to take a moment to absorb this, pulling out her monogrammed kerchief to pat at her eyes before speaking again.

"You do not have any predilections towards medicine, do you, Portia?" Mrs. Jones asked.

I shook my head at the sudden change of subject. "No, I have not. As I told you on the ship, ever since I was a little girl I had thought of law as a career that interested me, though I had no means with which to pursue my studies in that."

"King's College offers studies in law," she mused. "And I suppose those are the two compulsions in your blood — medicine and an overwhelming moral drive towards justice."

She snorted at the end of this sentence, and then, catching my eye, added, "Oh, not that I am laughing at the dead, my dear, but your grandparents were just *so* earnest about right and wrong. You really must correct that in yourself if it turns out to be an inherited trait. Most unappealing."

I laughed aloud, and after a moment, she joined me.

CHAPTER FOUR

I spent the next three weeks learning all I could about my famous grandfather, filling my lonely hours with this new family member.

I knew of course that this was a very emotional reaction to the loss of my mother and the hurt at her keeping this secret from me. Over and over I asked myself why she had felt the need to keep her father's name hidden from me. I knew how much it had frustrated her that her own mother was so secretive about it, so it would seem logical that she would want to spare her own child that frustration.

Were other truths being kept from me? Other family secrets that I deserved to know? I was alone in the world, with no real purpose, and no one to come home to. Keeping myself busy learning about my newly discovered relations meant less time spent sadly staring out the window missing my old life. I would fill my empty heart with as much data as I could about Dr. John Watson.

To do so, I read every one of his handwritten journals cover-to-cover, one right after another in chronological order. I paused only long enough to walk the streets and get to know my new city (maps were a favorite subject of mine, and I pinned several to the walls of my new apartment with small brass thumbtacks).

The map next to my front door was one of the subways and inner streets of the downtown core and was posted on a corkboard I had brought with me from Toronto. It allowed me to stick pins in the places I had been and mark the places I wanted to investigate next.

Upon reading the journal that included the casebook entitled "The Adventure of the Illustrious Client", I set out to see the west-end restaurant where Holmes had been attacked: the Café Royal. The French restaurant was everything I imagined it would be from Watson's description, situated on Regent Street and flanked by private members' clubs and other fine restaurants. I stood on the sidewalk looking in, imagining the scene described in the journal, rubbing my hands together in the March cold.

The map of southern England was more for reference than actual travel, and that I pinned to the wall behind my bed for the same reason my mother had hoarded all those travel brochures — as a little expression of ambition toward travel. Now that I was here, I might as well explore my new home country.

To read the journals, though, was as much an education on Dr. Watson as it was on Sherlock Holmes. The depth of trust and friendship between these two men was obvious and warmed my heart even as the hearth we had all shared in different centuries warmed my body.

I digested case after case voraciously and searched for corroborating material in the textbooks and written notes on the shelves. The number of mysteries these two had solved in their seventeen years together was amazing: everything from murders to grand theft, and working for royalty and chimney sweeps alike.

It was no longer a consideration to sell the townhouse at Baker Street. Quite on the contrary, this discovery had given me new purpose — learning about my famous family — and a new source of income that I could not overlook. I met with Mrs. Jones' accountant to work out a reasonable budget for myself and discovered that with my guardian covering my tuition costs, the income from my downstairs tenants would be more than enough to cover my small expenses. I owned the townhouse outright as passed down through my family, so my expenses were a very short list.

Being surrounded by the writings of my grandfather somehow made the loneliness more bearable. It connected me to my heritage despite being thousands of miles away from my homeland. Slowly I was starting to forgive my mother for hiding this from me. I might never know all her reasons, but my faith in her love for me meant that I gave her the benefit of the doubt.

One morning I found myself staring off into space, rubbing my silver cross, and I came to a simple conclusion: this family here in England had caused my mother pain. I wasn't sure how, or why, but it made the most sense based on the evidence. Perhaps she felt rejected. Or perhaps her mother had managed to pass on her adamant denials of this relationship. Whatever the underlying psyche, the discovery of John Watson as her hitherto unknown father did not bring her joy. She would have shared joy. She would have hidden pain.

Mrs. Jones flitted in and out of the apartment delivering clothes one day, bouquets the next, never staying long enough to answer a question unless she demanded my company at dinners and parties, where I was one of many guests.

At one such party, held at a home that was more marble than brick, I allowed Mrs. Jones to introduce me to the hosts and then quickly excused myself to find refreshments. Mrs. Jones gave me a look that conveyed her displeasure without a word, but I ignored it, making a beeline to the silver-laden buffet table. Waiters in smart white uniforms stood ready to serve out tiny bite-sized *hors d'œuvres* onto fine china. I shook my head at the waiter offering something gray on a cracker, pasting a smile on my lips and looking over at Mrs. Jones.

Seeing that her back was turned, I scampered away from the table to the window, where I could stand casually hidden by the velvet curtains. It was here that I spent most of these large engagements, regardless of the venue, watching the upper class toast each other and make merry. Only when I would see my guardian start looking around for me with her gray eyebrows knit in what I knew to be annoyance would I rejoin the party, so that she would find me smiling and enjoying myself with someone I had introduced myself to minutes before.

I will admit that I didn't try very hard to mingle amongst these people. Not only was I uncomfortable with the number of questions they invariably asked me, but I much preferred observation to socialization. Mrs. Jones never said a word about my activities, though, so I continued my efforts to hide even as she continued her efforts to show.

I was unrelenting in my efforts to quiz the older lady about our relationship, about her relationship with my grandparents, asking question after question to try to wrest even the smallest clue from which to unravel the secret that was Irene Jones. But she was deft in her artifice and skilled at turning the subject toward one more to her liking.

Brian Dawes was as well read on the case studies as I. He had spent weeks after my grandfather's death organizing the papers and books that had lain in disrepair for years in this upper apartment. We delighted in comparing our thoughts on the many cases we had both read and supplemented our readings with his stories from Scotland Yard, where he was in the last few months of training to become a constable.

"Have you come across the two cases written by Holmes?" Brian asked me on one of his upstairs visits as he uncovered the small plate of biscuits sent up by his mother. He was wearing a collared shirt with an old brown vest over top, and his hair was shorter today, probably cut in the style of his fellow constables.

I could tell that he had been at the shooting range earlier despite the wet hair that signaled a recent shower. The trousers and vest were fresh but the collared shirt still bore signs of gun grease and the smell of powder.

I took one of the biscuits with a smile. "Indeed, 'The Adventure of the Lion's Mane' and 'The Adventure of the Blanched Soldier', I believe they are called." I strode over to the bookshelf, taking a bite of the biscuit as I did so, the smells and taste of ginger flooding my senses. I choked slightly on the extreme flavor, and to my embarrassment, Brian clapped me on the back a few times before I could take a breath and thank him, my cheeks red.

"They are ... very good," I managed to squeak out as he quickly retrieved a small rag from my kitchenette.

"I call them Glaringly Ginger Biscuits, but we could rename them Garroting Ginger ... or Great Scott Ginger — what do you think would be a fairer warning to the unprepared?" he asked, his dimples

41

deep and his smile wide. I had knelt down to retrieve biscuit bits from the floor and took the rag with thanks before rising to return to the bookshelf for the journal we had been discussing.

I pulled it out and handed it to him as I carried the rag back to the dustbin. "I think a good start is to tell your hapless victim any of those names before they take a bite."

His grin grew wider, if possible. "But what fun would that be?"

I rolled my eyes, returning to our original topic. "Holmes may have been the superior detective of the pair, but I believe my grandfather far exceeded him in storytelling prowess," I said, trying to regain my composure.

I shook the rag out over the dustbin and turned back toward Brian, who had opened the journal. "I entirely agree," said he, looking up from the book to nod, his wide-set eyes wrinkling at the corners as they did when he was amused. "I miss your grandfather's voice in these cases."

I folded and unfolded the rag as he continued to skim the journal, unsure where to take this conversation next. Before he had come upstairs I had been quite busy looking over the list of textbooks recommended by King's College and had been annoyed by the knock at the door. But now I was looking for reasons for Brian to stay, which I found strangely odd and unsettling.

For the first time in my life, I was developing a friendship — something my mother had constantly talked about, especially in the last few months of her life. From the time I was a small child I could remember being alone, even when in a crowd of children my age. My quiet nature and inquisitive observations seemed to put people on edge, and it became common for me to carry a few books everywhere we went, because even when my mother was laughing and talking with her friends, their children seemed to want nothing to do with me. As I grew older, I began to avoid social gatherings, both so that my introverted nature would not be obvious and because I found new people distracting and couldn't help staring at them. My poor mother eventually gave up trying to find friends for me and allowed me my strange habits.

All this made it doubly odd that Brian and I seemed to get along so well so quickly. We bonded over the cases he brought home and the documented ones I was painstakingly going over in my own apartments, his own profession making me jealous and at the same time appreciative that he was so open and sharing. I felt a little sad that my mother wasn't here to witness this development, knowing how happy it would have made her.

I had hoped he would be able to tell me if there were letters of correspondence between my grandmother and grandfather, but he did not know of any, and I couldn't find any in my further searches of the apartment.

I once asked my guardian about it and she dismissed the very idea with a snort. "Oh, I am sure that John was the more sentimental of your two grandparents, but the only person he deigned write to or about was his flat mate," she swept her hand over the bookshelves, "as evidenced by this shrine."

I worried that perhaps my mother had some kind of correspondence passed down to her by her own mother that now lay amongst piles of refuse in our reclaimed Toronto house, but quickly decided that Constance Adams would not have passed any such items on to her daughter. She had spent her entire life denying her ex-husband's existence; she would not have changed that view even at the end of her life.

That left me with more and more questions about this family I knew so little about, and even more determined to investigate it through Dr. Watson's connections here in London.

CHAPTER FIVE

During one ambitious excavation, I managed to climb up into one of the attic storage spaces. Mrs. Dawes had advised against it: "Nothing up there but spiders 'n' dust!"

As usual, my curiosity won out. Borrowing a stepladder from downstairs, I made my ascent. Moving carefully, I pulled out my battery-powered flashlight (a gift from Mrs. Jones) and scanned the attic. The dust was absolute on the wooden floor, undisturbed but for a few tiny paw prints that appeared between items and disappeared under furniture.

The floor was creaky but seemed stable based on the weight of the contents. I could not stand in this space, the height being less than four feet, and therefore I was forced to crawl through flotsam stacked all around me. I shuddered when I encountered the well-chewed papers, wondering what did the chewing and promising myself to get some mousetraps next time I was out. I negotiated on my knees around cobweb-covered trunks, bags and all manner of old, broken furniture.

The air up here was well beyond musty. I ducked down to get several gulps of clean air before trying again. Tucking back up, I grabbed a random leather satchel and hauled it back down with me, closing the pulley door as soon as I got clear.

"Doing some dusting, dear?" the familiar melodic voice of my guardian said from somewhere below me.

I continued my descent, brushing at the cobwebs and dirt clinging to my hair. "Just exploring." I held aloft the leather satchel.

Her eyes lit up with recognition at the sight of it. I wondered again with annoyance how she knew so much about this townhouse, a question she had yet to answer despite my asking at least once a week.

She was removing her fur coat — this one mink, I believe — and wore an expensive day suit beneath, its lavender color bringing out the hazel in her eyes. She pulled off her long gloves and I noticed her jewelry and makeup, which were both heavier than usual for so early in the day, and glanced at her shoes, which were not at all suited to the snow.

I walked over to the desk. "Do you know this bag? Was it my grandfather's?"

She tilted her head to the side. "Yes, I believe so."

Excited now, I unfastened the clasps and pulled open the bag by the handles. Inside, I found the most unexpected articles: some jars of dried-up makeup, two wigs, a scarf, three pairs of eyeglasses and what looked like a fake nose.

"Extraordinary," I said.

"No," corrected Mrs. Jones, looking over my shoulder into the open bag. "Just a normal day at 221B Baker Street."

She chuckled, but it didn't sound happy — it sounded sad and bitter, as she sometimes did when referring to the past occupants of this apartment.

"I must be going now, dear," she announced airily. "I'm attending the opera this afternoon."

"But you've only just come from the opera," I remarked, confused.

She stopped in the midst of pulling her gloves from her pockets. "What *can* you mean, Portia?" she said, her back to me.

What did I mean? I knew she had already been to the opera today — less than an hour ago, in fact. My mind whirred as I struggled to articulate my thoughts. "Your glasses, Mrs. Jones. I can tell you've been wearing your opera glasses for some time today already."

She turned toward me now, eyes slightly widened. "My opera glasses are in my purse," she corrected, a touch of frost creeping into her voice.

But I knew I was right, so I pressed on. "The creases where you press the glasses against your face — you can still see where the makeup has been slightly smeared. More so on the left than the right. So if I had to guess, I'd say you were sitting in the upper left balcony this morning, perhaps watching a dress rehearsal."

I was out of breath and strangely excited at the end of my statement.

"Anything else?" she invited, one perfectly sculpted brow raised.

I squinted in thought, and then released my breath. "No, that is all." I awaited her reprimand, as was the usual reaction from anyone subjected to my observations.

The corners of her mouth turned up in a wry smile. "Better and better. Your grandmother's looks and your grandfather's brains. A deadly combination, I must say."

CHAPTER SIX

Your grandmother and I became close when we were both divorced young mothers living in San Francisco," Mrs. Jones explained over a late cup of tea several weeks later.

"We were both divorced by men who were very alike, obsessed with their work. It was like mixing oil and water in both our cases, perhaps even more so in mine than in hers."

A knock at the door interrupted the discussion. Brian popped his head in. He had come straight upstairs from work, not even stopping at his flat downstairs to change out of his uniform, so I knew he had something exciting to share.

"Oh, 'scuse me ladies, I didn't know you were over, Mrs. Jones. I had some news to share with Miss Adams from downtown. It'll keep — I'll come back."

He gave me a wink and went back out the door.

We listened to his receding footsteps on the stairs, and then Mrs. Jones spoke. "He graduates soon as a constable, yes?"

I nodded.

"Most exciting," she said, looking as if it were anything but.

"So you had a child from your marriage as well, and you were living in San Francisco?" I said, drawing her back to our earlier conversation.

"Oh, yes, as I was saying, we were very close. Our children practically grew up together, and it wasn't until I had to leave the country—" She hesitated. "On business, of course, that we lost touch for a few years."

"On business?" I repeated, noting the slightly defensive way she said the words.

She waved her hand as she tended to when she refused to go into detail. "It seemed very important at the time, but in hindsight, it of course was not."

"And then ... then my son left to join that cursed war." Her eyes took on a harder sheen. She pulled in a deep breath. "He was killed in action. I ran away from everything and everyone I knew. I ran for years. It is one of the reasons I am so well-traveled, I suppose."

She reached into her bag for one of her monogrammed hankies. My heart stirred at the similarity of our circumstances, both her son and my father being lost in the war. But then again, many sons and fathers were lost in that war, on both sides of the conflict.

"By the time I allowed myself to communicate with my old life, your grandmother was dead, and your mother had moved to Toronto and married that odious gambler."

I felt a twinge of guilt, remembering the fights I had with my mother over my former stepfather, and pushed it away with effort. My mother's choice of a second husband had never made any sense to me, but who were we to judge so many years later? It was a very mature reaction, I felt, after years of contempt for my stepfather. But in light of all that had happened since my mother's death, it seemed like the distant past.

I did some quick calculations. "So then your son was about the same age as my parents?"

She nodded stiffly. "Indeed, though I lost touch, as I said, with your mother after..."

"After the war," I finished for her, my brow furrowed as a new thought occurred to me. I had opened up my mouth to ask the question when she rose, pointing to the bookshelf.
"Tell me, have you considered moving some of this furniture around?" she asked, testing the weight of the bookshelf slightly. "Just

because this is how it was arranged doesn't mean it has to remain this way..."

"I ... I honestly haven't thought about it," I replied, disappointed because I knew pushing her for more information today would be fruitless. She would just announce that she had somewhere else to be and be gone before I could argue.

"I don't believe I have ever seen the wall behind this bookshelf for example," she said, tapping at her bottom lip thoughtfully and pulling out book spines at random.

I watched her for a moment and then realized what she was looking for.

"I don't believe that a hidden alcove could exist against that wall, ma'am," I said dryly, pointing at the window. "That is, after all, an outer wall, and behind that bookshelf would have to exist at least eight to ten inches of brick, and that does not leave a lot of room for hidden space."

"Indeed," she remarked thoughtfully, and then shrugged as if the subject no longer interested her and began regaling me with a new story about the ladies luncheon she wanted me to attend.

CHAPTER SEVEN

I started at King's College the same week Brian Dawes became Constable Dawes. I was sorting through my new books with an ear cocked, listening for him to get home, and when he did, I leapt to my front door.

Looking down the stairs I watched his mother come out of her downstairs apartment to coo at her son's new uniform, complete with hat and badge. He glanced up the stairs and gave me a cocky salute, taking off his hat and running a hand through his thick brown hair before answering a question from his father, who had just entered the hallway to join his wife and son. I smiled back at Brian. His black uniform enhanced his lean, tall body, making him seem so much older than his twenty-four years.

King's College was part of Oxford University and about an hour away from Baker Street by tube. The red brickwork stood out on the street, and the array of windows was a favorite feature of the students who were lucky enough to attend. Though I had only visited this school in the dead of winter, the headmistress, Mrs. Darbishire, assured me that the gardens in the summer were unparalleled. It was she whom my guardian had contacted about my entry into the college, though they didn't act like friends when we arrived on campus the first time. Indeed, Darbishire was a great deal friendlier toward me than to Mrs. Jones.

But unlike Mrs. Darbishire, my classmates seemed wholly unimpressed with me, as demonstrated by their giggling comments about my attire (old-fashioned) and 'colonial accent'.
These girls seemed to be rich, entitled and only mildly interested in the lessons we all attended. The few girls who were of my quieter,

anti-social disposition avoided me for exactly the personality traits that made us alike. As I had when attending classes in Toronto, I refused to allow either their disinterest or their derision to upset me, and I was actually glad for a moment that my mother would not be hurt on my behalf by their rejection. When my professors found out from the headmistress about my famous residence and the reason I lived there, they had many questions and many nice things to say about my late grandfather. Unfortunately, their attention did nothing to improve my reputation amongst my peers.

"This weekend, I want you all to read very carefully the chapter on chain of evidence," Professor Archer said, looking around the room at each of us, missing the rolled eyes from the back row of tittering debutants who had been whispering about the fashion faux pas at a recent ball they had all attended. "We'll have a little debate on it Monday morning, so I expect you to be experts in it."

The professor was of medium build with a small chin, a long gray-blond handlebar moustache, pale blue eyes covered by thick spectacles, and was probably five foot seven in height. Today he wore a bright green tie under his homemade vest, though his trousers were from his police uniform.

His gaze landed on me, his eyes lighting up, and my heart sank even before he said, "You might want to stop by Miss Adams' home if you are looking for inspiration — after all, I hear her grandfather filled bookshelves with notes on evidence and cases. I am sure Miss Adams wouldn't mind at all."

I winced as I looked around the room at the stony faces now directed my way.

Miss Wellesley, one of the most popular girls in the school, at least according to her own repeated declarations, put up her hand.

"Yes, Miss Wellesley?" Archer said.

"Oh, professor, I just wanted to say that," she feigned hesitation here, her dyed red curls framing her face in the latest short style seen on Hollywood starlets. I looked around at her friends, who were covering their grins with their hands as she spoke. "My mother doesn't feel comfortable with me attending a home without any sort of parents or even chaperones around. I mean, Miss Adams is living alone in that ... flat, after all."

She turned her sly green eyes my way, and I rolled my own, not even trying to hide my annoyance. The purse she carried around showed signs of repair while the leather strap was not the original, meaning that she had owned this very expensive purse for longer than the season it was in style. Her hair was dyed with a cheaper solution than was found in beauty salons, as evidenced by the lingering smell of henna and the stains I sometimes saw on her fingernails from doing the job herself.

All of this told me that for someone who acted high and mighty, her family fortune was not what it once had been, and certainly not at the level of the girls who followed her around hanging on her every word.

Archer looked taken aback by her statement, but he said nothing as she gave me a dismissive wave and led her pack of followers out of the classroom. Archer turned toward me, and I just nodded at him, gathering up my things as well. Professor Archer was also Chief Inspector Archer at Scotland Yard, and he was one of my biggest supporters at the college through his admiration for both Watson and Holmes. I knew he didn't mean to further alienate me by pointing me out, but he seemed to do so at least once a week.

Regardless of my continued social pariah status, I loved everything else about attending classes and absorbed knowledge like a veritable sponge. The class on the basics of real estate law and the class on the intricacies of legal communication and jargon fascinated me equally, but by far my favorite class was the one about historical cases brought before real judges and real juries. The various trials of author Oscar Wilde, the romantic back story to the trial of the mutinous crew of the Veronica; case after case I ingested like a half-starved vagrant invited to a buffet. I would come home every night with homework, and when I finished it, I would dive back into the cases of my grandfather. It was like my days were filled with theory and my nights with history and reality.

Employing inductive and deductive reasoning was second nature to me, just a few steps beyond my natural observant nature. It was a combination of observation and knowledge that allowed a 'leap' of logic ... Mr. Holmes had the uncanny ability to make the leap sooner than those around him.

A degree in law could only be bolstered by a powerful investigative mind, and I was determined that I would not squander this opportunity handed down to me from my very genes through John Watson. What better way to develop myself in this field than to suck in all the knowledge and experience this room had to offer?

I already had the keen observational mind (or so I flattered myself). I simply needed to add to this the knowledge of crimes and law that was readily available around me in the books on the shelves and the daily newspapers I read every single day.

I followed stories from stunning crime to eventual solution, making my own notes and cutting out articles to paste into my notebooks. When a crime went unsolved for weeks, I would badger Brian Dawes for details, determined to prove myself worthy of my newly discovered ancestral heritage. If I did that, maybe I could stop thinking about my mother and the years she spent alone after losing my father and then her mother. Even when she remarried, she spent most of her time with me, her new husband quickly returning to his old habits of drinking and gambling after their marriage. Maybe some distance from thinking about my mother's motivations would allow me to better understand her. By walking in her father's footsteps for a while I might, through a different route, come to understand why she didn't pursue their relationship, even after discovering who he was.

"Mrs. Jones?" I asked one evening as we sat in front of my fireplace.

"Mmm?" she replied, shaking herself awake from her light slumber in the wingback chair next to mine.

"Was there something wrong with Dr. Watson?" I asked, leaning forward so that my elbows were on my knees. "And by wrong, I don't mean physically. I mean was there something about him that would make my mother not want to reach out to him?"

Mrs. Jones looked taken aback for a moment. "John Watson was a gentleman, Portia, a doctor with a spotless reputation and a kindness I have described to you in detail. I'm not sure where you could be getting this idea from that there was something wrong with him."

I leaned back, a little frustrated. "There has to be a reason my mother chose not to get in contact with him once her mother died."

She shrugged, leaning toward the fireplace with the poker. "As I've said before, speculating about your mother's motivations is a waste of time. I think it's far more important to focus on you, and now, than on her back then."

"Do you think she felt rejected?" I asked, wrapping my arms around myself at the thought. "That maybe my grandfather didn't want her. Or didn't want us?"

Mrs. Jones sighed loudly, drawing my attention back to her face. "See, this is exactly what I was talking about — this obsession with dwelling on people who are dead and gone, and whose actions are now irrelevant..."

She trailed off and I started to feel a little foolish. Maybe I *was* dwelling in the past. Maybe my new guardian was right.

"I would hate for this obsession to become a driving force in your life, Portia," she continued, adjusting herself more comfortably in her chair. "Is it the study of law that is reminding you so much of Watson? Or is it these rooms? Because the college has a very convenient dormitory if you prefer. It is very early in your education, you know. We have plenty of time to reconsider your focus. There is, I believe, a program in literature — you do so love to read. Or botany?"

My head snapped up at that. "Oh, no, ma'am, that is entirely unnecessary. Honestly, I am so thankful that you are providing me the financial ability to attend the college, and I am perfectly happy to be living here. Really I am."

She waved her hands in that way she had, the palms soft and wrinkly even in the firelight. "Don't be silly, my girl, I only seek to provide you with options, not directives. If this is what you want to do, to be a lawyer, to work in the legal field, I am with you. But I suggest that you focus your attention on that present situation lest it be distracted by ghosts from the past. We have both, after all, been witness to your dips into depression..."

She was right in that, of course, and I colored at her observation, made after only knowing me for a few months. Once in a while I would find myself distracted from whatever was capturing my attention, and it was at those moments that memories of my mother would overtake me, like milk simmering on the stove that goes from a light bubble to spilling over the sides at a fast boil. In the same way the sadness would overflow out of me and I fought hard against it, as did Mrs. Jones in her own way.

I looked up at her beautiful face in the flickering firelight. She was incredibly intelligent, evidenced both by her perfect memory and her own keen sense of deduction. More often than not, when I would speak excitedly about a crime currently in the newspapers, she would quickly shred my solution with a few well-thought-out arguments.

Far from discouraging me, her intelligent debates drove me to work harder. I should be cognizant of her encouragement toward my education and more thankful of her efforts.

"You are right, of course," I said, taking a deep breath at her answering smile of approval. "I will focus on the future you have secured for me."

In my head, I swore to prove myself worthy of my mother's faith in me, of my lost father's memory, and of the ghost of my grandfather in this very room.

I didn't yet allow myself to put a name to this destiny; the very act of thinking of myself as an aspiring 'detective' felt arrogant at this point. But I promised myself at that moment to focus my learning, my actions and my very thoughts toward this unspoken goal.

Brian's time was taken up with a rash of local burglaries, so, naturally, my attention swung that way in terms of research. I separated out some of Holmes and Watson's cases that were specifically about thievery and made copious notes on them, also referencing my legal books and changes to laws since my grandfather's time.

The constabulary's continued frustration with the unsolved cases kept my interest high, and I spent hours on the streets of London, walking from one crime scene to another. The smoke from the exhaust of the cars combined with the breath of the people walking the sidewalks in this winter season, but the traffic and the types of traffic varied, and I noted it all. Unlike Toronto, which was a very new city when compared to the one I now lived in, London had distinct populations, smells, activities and yes, even tastes when you traveled from one borough to another. The smells of detergent and cleaning solvents assailed me as I walked around Acton as surely as the smell of fish heralded my arrival in Barking. I took the tube to most of my destinations, but walked home for hours once I had my fill of the sights, often stopping to stare up at stately buildings or to peer into the dusty windows of closed-down shops. Surely I must have looked mad to the Londoners who passed, but I cared not; it made me feel even closer to Watson and Holmes as I tried to imagine what they would have done were they on the case.

Determined to learn more than could be gleaned from textbook and diary, I once again made a visit to the dusty old attic above my apartment. Finding a ratty old suit and beard, I disguised myself as an old man with a huge nose. Consulting some of Holmes's notes, I reduced the size of the nose ("the key to anonymity is to have no distinguishing features by which you might be remembered").

Turning this way and that in the mirror, I found something was missing. I grabbed one of my simple frocks and stowed it under my shirt so that I looked as though I had a slight belly. Perfect!

I carefully left 221 Baker Street, trying to disguise my exit, and hailed a horse-drawn hackney. My notes indicated that although the burglaries seemed to occur at random spots in the city, two had resulted in a chase, and the chases had both ended down near the river. The robberies were starting to form a pattern: four in the last thirty-four days, and there hadn't been one yet this week, so this seemed a good night to test out my theories.

I intended to stake out a spot on Westminster Bridge, just south of Scotland Yard, where both of those chases had taken place. From there I would be able to hear if an alarm was raised, and pursue my theory of a water-bound escape.

The driver let me off with barely a glance. I walked up and onto the bridge from the north side. Westminster sat on the north side of this bridge, with the borough of Lambeth to the south. I passed two alcoves that were already occupied, averting my eyes from a couple giggling and fondling each other in public. Finding a deserted alcove on the east side, I sat down, noting its dark gothic structure and feeling a tingle of foreboding that I quickly shook off.

"More likely than not, nothing will happen tonight," I whispered to myself as I shivered, half hopeful and half worried.
"I could come back here every night for the next week, and the thief could run down Waterloo Bridge instead."

People walked by, vehicles, horses, the usual traffic in a busy city. More than a few people looked at me and then quickly averted their eyes, enough of them staring to feed my insecurity that I had failed at my disguise, and I reddened under my makeup, holding the nose in place when the glue gave way. Fortunately, though I continued to elicit stares, no one stopped and actually spoke to me or demanded to know what I was about.

Hours passed, and my feet went numb. I began to lose my enthusiasm for this stakeout. It was after three in the morning by now, and no one had passed my pathetic vigil for an hour or so. I chided myself that this was a colossal waste of time, even as I encouraged myself to see out the bloody thing despite my increasingly failing disguise.

The glue from my fake nose and eyebrows had betrayed me and there was nothing I could do about that, having only two hands. I chose to focus on holding on to my nose, allowing the furry eyebrows to drop into the snow in front of where I sat, like two lost caterpillars that had somehow stayed alive past their summer lifetime.

I must have fallen asleep. I awoke to a splash and sprang up, despite my numbed limbs, my fake stomach falling at my feet in a tumbled heap. I cursed under my breath, scooped my rumpled clothing off the filthy cobblestones and squinted in the flickering lamplight. A figure was just exiting the west end of the bridge — he must have run right past me. What was that splash, though? A boat where his partner awaited the pass-off of the loot?

Excited, I leaned over the side of the bridge — nothing. I ran to the north side: again, nothing. I could see from here all the way to the Waterloo Bridge in the clear moonlight and nothing was on the water, not even a bird ... just the usual rubbish and floating debris that always seemed to litter the Thames. I returned to the south side of the bridge, still seeing nothing moving in the water, certainly no boats, and slapped the stone railing in frustration, causing my rolled up clothing to fall out of my shirt again.

Just then I heard voices coming in my direction from the far west end of the bridge. Quickly, I shoved my extra clothes under me and sat back down in my original spot, trying to feign a drunken slouch, just in time to watch two constables with a roughly dressed man between them, carrying on an animated discussion. The man was shackled at the wrists and had a determined smirk on his face as the constables heaped insults on him and cuffed him behind the ear.

"Finally slipped up, didn'tcha, old boy?" one officer said, elbowing the shackled man as they passed me without a second look.

He'd been caught! My shoulders slumped, dismayed that I had been so wrong. He was not using a boat for his escape at all; he was simply running across the bridge to get from wherever he had committed his crime to wherever his hideout was. Some detective I was!

They had barely left the bridge when a half-dozen other officers appeared, carrying whistles and yelling at each other to spread out.

I yawned, throwing the cursed fake nose over the side of the bridge and trudging toward home in defeat, leaving the police to their obviously successful work.

CHAPTER EIGHT

It had taken more than an hour to walk home, so the next day I woke late thankful it was a Saturday with nothing scheduled but a day of leisurely reading.

By the time I had dressed it was past eleven o'clock in the morning, and the family downstairs had left on their various errands for the day. With one hand I spooned a tiny amount of Mrs. Dawes' cold, congealed porridge I found in a pot on the stove into a bowl, and with the other flipped through today's paper. Landing on the story I had been seeking, I transferred food and paper to the table that I might more comfortably consume both.

My eyes widened as I read the details: "Suspect apprehended fleeing police, accomplice suspected," and most interesting of all, "stolen tiara still missing."

So they had caught someone, but was it the right someone? If it was, where was the stolen tiara? If it was the man from last night, he had run across the bridge and been caught on the other side. When did he have the chance to pass the necklace to an accomplice? I lowered the paper, deciding that I needed more data.

I was out the door and headed toward Scotland Yard within a half hour. My journey was marked by a churning brain as I mentally riffled through all available case notes I had memorized from my grandfather's collection. Without a confession or the stolen item they would have to release the suspect, and according to the papers, he was denying any involvement in the crimes.

The Yard, as it was colloquially known, had its rear entrance called Great Scotland Yard, an entrance I had been introduced to by one of my professors at the college who was also a well-respected chief inspector. I looked up at the building as I approached, its striped red bricks, Portland stone and elegant turrets reminding one of a modernized castle. It was designed by Norman Shaw and overlooking the Thames. I had read that it was a vast improvement over the original offices at Whitehall. I had visited them on one of my many forays into the city and agreed heartily with the improvement of space and architecture "New" Scotland Yard afforded its occupants.

"Good morning, Detective Chief Inspector," I said, recognizing Professor Archer speaking to a sergeant I did not know on the steps that led up from the street. The man he was speaking to made to step forward as I approached, and I nodded at him. I glanced back down at the street thoughtfully as my professor answered my greeting.

"Why, good morning, Miss Adams," he replied, tipping his hat genially, his freshly waxed moustache glistening in the sunlight.

"What brings you to our offices so early on a Saturday? Surely not more follow-up questions on the case study I assigned?"

"Research, sir. I read in the paper that the alleged jewel thief had been apprehended," I admitted, stopping to his side.

"Oh, no 'alleged' about it, ma'am," answered the sergeant, raising his chin at me.

"He has confessed, then?" I asked.

The sergeant's chin dropped back down, as did his eyes from my direct stare. "No, not yet, but we are confident that we will have a positive identification from the owner of the jewelry very soon. He was seen as he climbed out the bedroom window with his stolen goods!"

"Ah, that is damning indeed," I agreed. "And that is whose arrival you are awaiting, then, the owner of the stolen tiara?"

The sergeant started slightly and his mouth gaped. "How did you know that we were waiting for the witness to arrive?"

"I didn't, until you told me that there was a witness," I admitted, and then turned to point to the street. "But if I were to bring in a witness to the Yard, a witness that perhaps did not want her name in the paper, I would bring her in the rear doors. I would also avoid attention by sending two higher-ranking officers out to wait for her, because it would seem far below their station to be on lookout duty.

I would position those officers on the west side of the staircase, perhaps feigning enjoying a cigarette since you do not smoke, Professor, so that a hackney could quickly pull up, dislodge the patron and turn around without waiting for traffic, as there is so little on this side."

The sergeant looked incredulously from his still-smoking cigarette to my professor and back at me.

"Also, when I first approached, you tensed on the balls of your feet, as if my appearance excited you," I continued. "Since we had never met, I surmised that you were waiting for a woman of my age and description, and until the chief inspector identified me, you remained 'at the ready'."

My professor was by now grinning broadly and patted his stunned peer on the back. "She has some skills, our Miss Adams does. Granddaughter of the estimable Dr. Watson, did you know?"

"The late Dr. Watson of the detective offices of Sherlock Holmes?" the sergeant asked as I blushed.

"None other!" my professor boasted, and then turning to me, asked, "Though are you entirely sure of your parentage, Miss Adams? I knew Dr. Watson well, and as amiable and intelligent a man he was, your instincts are positively Holmesian!"

I preened under his compliment even as the sergeant seemed to be annoyed by it. "Harrumph. Holmes was brilliant, truly, but impossible to work with from what I hear. Not someone to emulate, young lady, if that is your plan."

I had opened my mouth to respond when the lady they had been waiting for pulled up in a cab. I stepped out of the way as they rushed down to escort the woman into the building. As she passed, I noted her expensive navy blue wool dress with its fashionable cap sleeves and her wide-set eyes under a remarkable bonnet with a familiar triangle-shaped clasp. I pegged her at about twenty-five years old and nodded at her as she was escorted past me and into the building.

CHAPTER NINE

Two days later, while we were helping his mother set the table, Brian admitted that the woman had been unable to make a positive ID of the suspect they had brought in, and that the man, a Mr. Ben Fawkes, had been released despite the police's continued belief in his guilt.

I took to walking home over that same bridge every day, noting that on Tuesdays and Sundays it was almost abandoned, as opposed to Fridays when traffic was at its highest as food and liquor made their way back and forth over its bricked surface. Traffic under the bridge seemed to be regular as well, with fishing boats and skiffs gliding under it with regularity, except on Sundays when the water was almost still with inactivity.

I tried to stay positive during those weeks, filling my time as best I could, but if I had any close friends, which I did not, I would have admitted to them that I felt very small in that huge city. Insignificant, an outsider and just ... small. Except when I was pursuing a clue or immersed in my grandfather's diaries — that was when I felt connected and part of a bigger legacy, and it was an addictive feeling.

Brian and I were becoming closer, but I felt like he couldn't possibly understand my loneliness, living with both his parents, able to visit his grandparents in Surrey whenever he wanted to, and having a full social life with the friends he had made at Scotland Yard. A few times I had to swallow past my jealous feelings — like when watching his mother give him a kiss on the top of his head as she walked by his chair at the dinner table. How could I tell anyone, even Brian, just how alone I was? I might have told Mrs. Jones, since she was the closest thing I had to family these days, but she was showing up less and less at Baker Street — a pattern I was too proud to question when she did actually stop by. After all, if she thought me mature enough to live on my own, perhaps it was a weakness in me to feel this isolated. I wouldn't allow for it.

Another week went by, punctuated by another robbery. Again jewelry was stolen, and again, according to the papers, the foot chase led down toward the river.

Brian confessed over dinner with his family that the police were at a loss. The items stolen and the times of day varied, as did the location of the robberies. The police believed that there were as many as five thieves working together to commit these crimes, based on the information they would require to both locate the items and to escape time after time.

"According to Mr. Holmes, though," I broke in over the roast, "a conspiracy of more than three is rare, and five would be totally unmanageable because of the basic tenets of criminals: greed and violence."

"I wholeheartedly agree, and yet the sergeant in charge of the case insists that only a band of criminals could successfully continue to steal and evade capture," Dawes replied, reaching for the roasted potatoes.

We all chewed in silence over this. Two I could perhaps see, but four or five? It did not seem likely.

"One point has not been released to the papers yet," Brian whispered conspiratorially so that his parents wouldn't overhear. "At least one of the items, the tiara, has reappeared on the black market — we believe it was sold to a Turkish millionaire. We are talking to the local authorities about it."

We both looked at his parents to see if they were listening, but their ears were attuned to the radio playing behind Mr. Dawes senior.

"Well, that is something, is it not?" I whispered back, turning this new fact over in my head for possible links.

"Yes and no. The sergeant had claimed the night that this Fawkes fellow was captured, he had thrown the tiara aside, which is why we found nothing on him. But we had a good six officers down there searching the whole route, even the river, within minutes of his capture, and nothing..."

I remembered seeing the squad of officers spread out on the bridge and beyond that night, so I nodded. "The question is, if Fawkes is the thief, then how did the tiara he stole that night get from him to a Turkish millionaire—"

"—without an accomplice?" finished Brian. "There's the rub. If it wasn't on him, and he didn't ditch it, he handed it off. That's Sergeant Michaels' theory.

*　　*　　*

Later that March week I was reminded again of the case when my guardian stopped by with her arms full of fabric.

"Gorgeous, are they not?" she exclaimed happily, laying out roll after roll on my paper-covered desk. "Pick one. I will have a fabulous new dress made for you for your birthday in July."

I flipped through them. "They are lovely, thank you for thinking of me. But wherever did you get them? I have not seen their like in London or in the States."

"Oh, I have my suppliers," she answered mischievously. "Oh! This blue one matches your eyes, hold this one up."

Obliging, I stood in front of the full-length mirror as she draped an azure silk over my shoulder and brushed my dark hair out over it. The silk was well suited to my tall frame and slim build, draping and hanging over me like a waterfall. With her standing behind me in the mirror I could imagine how she had looked at my age and remembered her words about how often she had remarried. She was not as tall as me and had a more womanly figure even at her age, but remarkably her skin was still her most beautiful feature.

"Have you been following the recent run of jewel heists in London?" I asked, eyeing a new turquoise ring she was sporting. It was striking, a gold band with a flower blossom of four turquoise stone petals all inlaid with silver. Another purchase from her suppliers? Where had I seen that style? My eyes wandered to one of the textbooks on Persian antiquities on the shelf.

"Hmm?" was her only answer as she refolded the blue and pulled out a vibrant pink shot with silver threads. I wrinkled my nose at it. "The stolen jewelry — the press has been calling those responsible the Gang of Thieves."

67

"Indeed?" she remarked, putting the pink over her own shoulder and turning this way and that in the mirror. I recognized her disinterest and changed the subject, though my mind stayed on the case. But when she left, I did pull out a few of those books on antiquity and tried to place where I had seen the design of that ring. I was heeding one of Mr. Holmes's tenets, to follow my instincts, and there was something about that ring that tickled some part of my brain.

*　　*　　*

The Sunday following her visit I was once again wandering the bridges, starting on Waterloo Bridge, with my dog-eared copy of the *Chronicles of Avonlea* in my hand. Having now walked across each bridge that crossed the river Thames in downtown London, I could attest that the view from this bridge were the most pleasing. The bridge runs from The Strand on the north side, above Victoria Embankment, over to the South Bank. I wandered there reading about Anne Shirley and the community of Avonlea for almost an hour in the failing light, the granite of the bridge fading from sunlit white to dark gray.

Finally, when it was too dark to read or make observations on the locals and traffic, I headed toward Westminster Bridge. Just as I placed my foot on the bridge, I was surprised to recognize a familiar face coming my way — Ben Fawkes.

Familiar to me, of course, because I had seen him that cold night on the bridge when I was so badly disguised as a vagrant. He took no notice of me as he crossed in the opposite direction in a great hurry, but before I could even begin to take in the details of his appearance, the most noxious smell assailed me.

Despite wanting to remain unnoticed, I had to cover my mouth and nose as he passed me, the odor was so pungent. As soon as he was a few feet behind me the smell thankfully receded. I hadn't remembered a smell that night on the bridge. Where *had* the man been lately to smell so horrible?

He gained the street I had just exited. I turned to casually hang over the bridge. He passed only one other person, but I could tell by the way the passerby turned slightly from his path that he too was affected by the stench.

I returned home and set to bathe immediately, wondering if I should add this detail to my notes on the case. I finished toweling my hair dry (even with a bit of lavender, I swore I could *still* smell that noxious stench), and throwing the towel over a chair to dry in front of the fireplace, I pulled out one of the many notebooks on the shelf. According to my grandfather, Mr. Holmes had insisted time and again that no detail was too small to overlook. He had documented instances where the famous detective had solved a case and then returned to clarify it when he made connection with a forgotten fact years later.

I therefore followed his lead. Inspired, I pulled open one of my grandfather's dog-eared medical books. Surely that horrible smell could be identified.

CHAPTER TEN

By the end of April another two robberies had been committed, with no further progress made by the investigating authorities to either regain the stolen objects or apprehend those involved. Brian confided in me that out of desperation the sergeant in charge of the case had hauled Fawkes in again for further questioning.

"Did you notice a smell when they brought him in?" I asked.

"A smell?" he repeated, looking understandably confused. "No, not that I recall. He was one cool customer, though. Smiled at us as he was brought into the station, even winked at the inspector."

That was interesting in itself. Surely an innocent man would be annoyed at being brought in twice for questioning for a crime he didn't commit. Then again, a guilty man should look scared or defensive at being brought in again. What did it say about a man who found the exercise amusing?

By now, the press had renamed the story to highlight the police's inability to catch the perpetrators, calling them the "Invisible Hand" and the "Unstoppable Gang." This was of course still based on Sergeant Michaels' own continued postulation that these crimes were being carried out by an organized group of thieves, something I still couldn't quite buy into.

I had a two-week break between classes, and since I had no homework and no more interesting cases, I decided to pursue a new angle rather than give in to the lingering feeling of isolation.

The name of the only eyewitness in the case was a highly guarded secret at the Yard, so much so that all my persuasive skills could not convince my professor to divulge it, for fear that the witness would be in danger from the gang. Nor could Brian glean the information on my behalf, so I looked back at my notes from the day. As we had passed each other on those stairs, I had noted that the flustered woman frequented the same hat maker as my guardian. The clasp on the side of her hat bore the same triangular stamp of a well-known London milliner.

I headed downtown. In the millinery, I made some small talk with one of the ladies behind the counter before describing the hat I had seen.

"Oh yes, that was a special order for Madame LaPointe of Archer Hall. I remember it well," she assured me. "Green velvet with a hawk-feather bouquet. Really a one-of-a-kind creation."

I thanked her kindly and took the next cab to Archer Hall in Hampstead Village. The grounds included an orchard that had been winterized by the staff, the trees wrapped in burlap and rope to ward off the worst of the winter chill.

After ringing the doorbell, I was ushered into the stately home by the butler. I looked around in awe at the combination of oriental and English décor, the rugs from some Eastern country — either Afghanistan or Pakistan, by the pattern, though I could not be positive in my identification. Moments later he delivered me to a fine sitting room, and the very lady I sought entered to greet me. She was dressed this time in a long pink wool skirt with a small jacket that complimented it perfectly, her walk graceful and silent on her thick rugs.

"Madame LaPointe, I presume," I said, offering my hand, forcing my eyes to meet hers instead of cataloguing the furniture and accessories.

"Yes," she answered in a lilting French accent. "Do I know you?"

"Not really," I admitted, and explained our brief encounter on the steps to Scotland Yard, and the actions I had taken to find her.

She took a seat, crossing her slippered feet, looking only marginally less confused. "*Alors,* you came all this way *seulement* to see if my jewelry had returned?" Her brow furrowed.

"Not exactly, though if you tell me it had, I should be most pleased for you," I answered.

She sadly shook her head.

I continued. "I was hoping to hear more about the theft, Madame LaPointe. You see, I am studying law — in my first year, at King's College, and this case has fascinated me."

"Ah, I see. *Dommage,* there is not much for me to say," she replied, settling back on her golden-flowered settee. "But what I told the police, I can also tell you: I was at the church. It is very close to here. I was helping to ... um, to organize for the choir practice, when one of the friends of mine, Madame Polk, arrived. I was reminded I had borrowed a shawl from her the week before. I asked her to stay there while I ran back to the house to bring it back for her. I left, ran back into my house and straight up the stairs and to my bedroom where the shawl, I knew it was there.

"I passed none on my way in the door or up the stairs. Later I found out that James, my butler, was out walking with the dogs. And that Mary, my maid, she was at the kitchen. *Alors,* I ran straight to my room and had my hand on my shawl when *quel que* ... something made me look towards my window. There I saw a man almost out on the sill, half out and half in, with a sack in his hand."

I was taking notes as she spoke and wrote for a few seconds after she stopped speaking to catch up.

"Well?" she asked as soon as I lifted pen from paper, her brown eyes on mine.

"How did you realize what had been stolen?"

"*Mon dieu*, I screamed, and he, the man, he leapt the rest of the way out of the window and he was gone from my sight," she answered. "I must have frozen in the shock for a moment because the next thing, Mary was beside where I was, asking me what was wrong."

"And then?"

"And then we both of us ran to my jewelry cabinet and to discover that my mother's tiara was taken."

I looked up from my notes. "Only one piece was stolen?"

"*Mais oui*," she answered, nodding, "the very most precious piece of jewelry I own."

"But surely the rest of your jewelry is worth quite a lot of money as well," I mused. "And how could the thief had known that the tiara was the most valuable thing in your cabinet? Why not take it all?"

"Sergeant Michaels, he believes that I ... interrupted? Interrupted the man in the middle of his burglary, which is why he got away with so little," she offered. "The sergeant, he said that if I had returned even a half hour later, *comme* the choir practice would end, I would have lost everything."

"But he was already halfway out your window when you entered the room," I answered, dismissing the theory. "Were you wearing the same type of shoes you are wearing now?" I pointed with the end of my pencil at her fine little slippers.

She nodded.

"I doubt he even heard you coming with those light slippers," I continued. "I would guess that you surprised him as he was trying to leave, not as he was picking through your valuables, meaning he got what he came for and the rest of your jewelry for some reason didn't interest him."

She didn't answer, perhaps digesting my words.

"Did you wear the tiara out recently?" I asked, tapping that same pencil against my lips. "Perhaps to an event that got press coverage? Exposing it to the public?"

She shook her head. "*Non*, not for over a year have I worn that piece, it is quite large, after all."

"But then why just for the tiara? And if that was all he wanted, why was he carrying a sack?" I asked. "How big was the sack, do you think?"

"*Grand*. Bigger than my purse, and it looked full already," she answered after a moment's thought.

"Full?" I repeated. "Full of what? Surely he wasn't going from house to house collecting jewelry? Was anything else of yours missing? Perhaps something other than jewelry?"

"I think it is not, we did a very good check through my things and police then did as well."

I nodded, my mind whirling. "Thank you so much for your time, Madame. I do appreciate it."

She stood. "*Pas de problème*, Miss Adams."

I followed her out of the room, but as I made to pull on my gloves, I found I had one last question: "Madame LaPointe, what made you turn towards the window? Did you hear a sound?"

She paused thoughtfully. "*Non*, and I confess, when I tell to the police about my finding that man in my rooms, they really didn't think it important..."

I raised my eyebrows.

"It was this *mauvais* smell, Miss. Adams," she whispered. "This horrible, rotten smell!"

CHAPTER ELEVEN

The following week Mrs. Jones found me sitting on the floor in front of my fireplace surrounded by notes and books. She had thrown out the threadbare rug that had sat there for decades the week before, with promises to replace it with a "more suitable one." So I had folded up one of the blankets from my bed and sat on that instead.

"My goodness!" she exclaimed as she took in the spectacle.

I couldn't blame her, really. I must have looked a sight — and the room looked like a tornado had swept through it with photos of my mother, my grandfather's old papers, and half-eaten meals and empty mugs and glasses scattered all over.

She marched straight to the window and yanked open the heavy drapes, surprising me with the brightness of the sun.

"When did you last leave this room?" she demanded, struggling to open the window a crack, succeeding only when she put down her cane and used both hands.

"Yesterday morning." I yawned. She turned toward me with a raised eyebrow, so I gave in. "Maybe it has been a few days. I actually don't recall, exactly. What day is this?"

"Monday, and we are going out, so get dressed," she announced, shaking her head.

Something I had almost immediately discovered about my guardian was that she could be very bossy, and within a half hour she had bullied me into a bath and then into the new clothes she had brought for me. They consisted of a dark wool skirt that I knew even before touching it would itch, a pair of annoying stockings that were destined to slowly slouch down my legs, plus a cream blouse with shoulder pads that made me look like an American football player. The only redeeming item was a pair of brown leather gloves that were so soft they felt like I was wearing velvet rather than animal skin. Regardless of my discomfort, another half hour later found us walking toward the market to find some fruit and to take some air.

"Your professors tell me that you show amazing promise," she said as we shared a bag of roasted chestnuts.

"I appreciate their kind regard," I murmured, my sleepy brain still gnawing at the case spread all over my sitting room floor.

"Yes indeed, their letters speak of excelling in writing, leading the class in debates and having a remarkable memory for detail and law," she continued as we strolled amongst the various stalls.

She stopped at a grocer's cart, picking delicately through some old-looking apples before waving away the hopeful merchant.

"They seem to be drawing interesting linkages between your skills and your ancestry," she offered, eyes slanted.

"For which I am flattered," I answered, following my guardian to another stall, this one with various kinds of animals laid out on butcher blocks and hanging from wooden struts.

"An interesting leap, in my view," she snorted. "Your intelligence is your own and, I believe, independent of who your mother and father were, don't you think? Surely we are our own individuals, destined to make our own mistakes and create our own successes."

Unfortunately for Mrs. Jones, I was no longer able to answer. I had halted, almost mid-step, seized mentally and physically by something clicking into place.

"Good heavens, Portia!" she exclaimed when I didn't answer and she turned to see why not.

I don't know what she saw at that moment, but I felt as though my hair were standing on end. Like I had touched an electric wire and was frozen in place by the current still running through me.

"Portia!" she said again, now shaking my arm.

"That smell..." I finally managed to gasp.

"The smell?" she answered, surprised. "Come over here, then." She guided me by the elbow toward a small garden within sight, away from the stalls.

"Now, take a few deep breaths, get your—" she was saying reassuringly when I interrupted.

"That's the smell. That's what he smelled like — rotten meat!"

"What? Who?" she replied, confused.

"And I bet if I ask Madame LaPointe, she'd recognize it as well," I blathered on, barely hearing her in my excitement.

"Madame LaPointe? What has she to do with any of this?" Mrs. Jones asked, her tone exasperated.

I could not explain without revealing my evening visits to the bridge, so I made my apologies to my poor guardian, who by now was looking quite confused, and we continued on our walk as best we could, my mind focused on my case.

Smithfield Market was only two miles from Guy's Hospital, where I knew the department of forensics was located as part of the University of London. Coercing my guardian south across London Bridge towards Southwark, I managed to escape with promises of attending a charity ball in a few weeks.

I had to agree to a fitting for a new dress, and finally, with a kiss and a self-satisfied smile, Mrs. Jones hailed a cab and left me to walk the rest of the way to the hospital on my own.

I had never been inside this building before, but the signage was very helpful, directing me to the large library in the basement appropriately situated next to the teaching morgue. I pushed open the door marked 'Library', noting that the smell in here owed much to the antiseptic in the morgue opposite and borrowed equally from the temperature requirements — it being noticeably cooler down here than on the main floor.

"May I help you, miss?" a high-pitched voice asked as I looked round at the many bookshelves and tables in the dimly lit room. The voice belonged to a tiny older woman who couldn't have been more than five feet tall, but with commanding thick eyebrows over equally thick spectacles. I guessed her age at between fifty and sixty, and she wore a blue and orange tartan shawl around tiny shoulders, the pin holding it in place bearing the letters RMA.

"Yes, thank you," I replied, pulling off my gloves and extending my hand. "My name is Portia Adams, and I am a law student at King's College."

She tilted her graying head instead of shaking my hand, replacing one of the books in her arms on a shelf. "Is that so? Is that she-bear Mrs. Darbishire still stalking the halls of your college these days?"

I fought down a grin at her characterization, visualizing my heavy-set headmistress with the unfortunate chin hairs. I knew that before taking on the top position at the college, Darbishire had worked in the library, perhaps explaining her relationship with this woman. The woman caught the quirk of my lips and gave a toothy grin. "Ay, I see that she is. M'name's Cotter, and I'm the librarian here. What is it you couldn't find at King's that brings you here? I worked those stacks many years ago. They boast some of the best collections this side of Oxford."

"True, though not as good as the ones at Sandhurst," I commented, smiling when her eyes widened and her hand drifted up to touch the pin on her shawl emblazoned with the colors of the well-known military school. I nodded before saying, "Your son, I presume?"

"Yes," she replied, looking down at the pin and then back up at me, her shoulders rising as she spoke from a place of pride, "he's head boy for the second year in a row."

My deduction concerning her 'darling boy' bought me a quiet corner in the library and the personal attention of the person who knew it best.

Quickly I described what I was looking for and with her help was soon surrounded by thick medical textbooks, books on veterinary medicine, forensics and anatomical drawings. Mrs. Cotter offered a cushioned chair from behind her own desk for me to use at the large square table with a reading lamp before I dove into the books.

I was most interested in the science of what happens to a body directly after it dies — its first moments, hours and days of being a corpse. I glanced up from my comfortable position toward the glass doors that led out of the library and to the only other rooms down here: the morgue. Once the body cooled and the blood coagulated, what happened next?

I flipped through book after book, borrowing a pad of paper from Mrs. Cotter to scrawl notes, fascinated by the stages of decomposition and foment that every living thing underwent after death and how exact the schedule was. How soon rigor mortis set in. How quickly the body rotted.

"Stepping out for a bite, luv, can I get you anything?" Mrs. Cotter asked, making me jump since I had not heard her step so close. She already had her coat and gloves on as she looked at me expectantly, her eyes on a level with mine for the first time because she was standing and I was still seated.

"Oh, no thank you, Mrs. Cotter, is it all right if I stay?" I replied, putting down my borrowed pencil and flexing my hand, only now realizing that it was aching. I glanced at the clock above the doorway, surprised to see it was already five o'clock in the evening.

She shrugged. "Just don't leave while I'm out, and you can stay as long as you want," she replied with a wink. "I'll be back within the hour."

I smiled as she tottered off, glancing down at my notes and then back up as I heard a voice that I thought I recognized through the open door. With a frown, I stood, groaning as I did so, feeling the effects of sitting for hours, and walked toward the door still swinging slowly shut.

"No, I tell you, we nicked him square in the middle of his..."

"Constable Dawes?" I said, my hand still on the library door so it did not lock behind me, but my eyes on the three uniformed gentlemen standing in the hallway.

"Miss Adams?" he replied, turning my way with surprise stamped on his handsome face.

I grinned and he grinned back as he and his two comrades removed their hats and said their hellos. Introductions were made all around and I learned that they were dropping off a body at the morgue.

"Poor bugger froze, we think," Constable Bonhomme, a young man in his twenties, explained. His sideburns were a touch longer than fashionable. "Brought 'im in for Beans t'take a look at, though."

"Beans?" I asked, looking quizzically at the three men, who all laughed, only Brian looking chagrined.

"It's our nickname for Dr. Beanstine, one of the Yard's coroners, Miss Adams," he said, elbowing his friend in the ribs to get him to stop smiling so broadly. "It's all in good fun, I swear."

I was invited for a drink at the pub with the three of them but begged off, citing the work I was already neck-deep in, and shook hands with them each in turn, smiling at Brian as he turned back at the stairs leading to the main level.

Feeling a good deal warmer than I had a few moments ago, I returned to my lonely work, pulling my chair up to the table and focusing on the dog-eared copy of *Gray's Anatomy.*

Mrs. Cotter returned at some point, popping by my desk to take a pile of books I had already reviewed and delivering a few more as we refined my search more and more. The grisly images in the books were detailed with captions and surrounded by tables of real data from experiments, and I took careful note of everything I could.

"You're still here?" said Brian, surprising me for the second time that evening. I looked over my shoulder to find him standing right behind me, staring curiously down at my pad of paper.

I rubbed my eyes wearily before answering, "Why? What time is it?"

"It's after nine," he replied, leaning over my shoulder to put his finger on my pad. "And what in the world is bloat?"

"It's a stage of decomposition," I replied, smelling the beer on his breath and feeling it warm the nape of my neck. I swallowed nervously. "I thought you were out with your mates?"

"I thought I'd make sure you got home all right," he replied with a dimpled smile, leaning in even closer to whisper into my ear. "Besides, I think your chaperone has been asleep for a half hour."

It took me a few seconds to pull my attention away from his lips at my ear over to the desk, where I could see Mrs. Cotter slumbering with her feet up on a patterned ottoman.

He laughed softly, stepping away from me to start collecting up the books scattered on the desk, allowing me a moment to catch my breath.

"This is rather specific research," Brian commented, his smile turning to a frown as he read the titles of the books as he picked each up. "For something at college?"

"No, actually — you did say that Fawkes was an assistant undertaker, did you not?" I replied, with a glance at my notes to make sure I had taken down the title of a book before adding it to the stack.

He looked taken aback but nodded. "So these are helping you to connect Fawkes to the robberies somehow?"

"He's an expert in dead bodies," I responded, "and now I think I have a better idea of just how much he understands, and how that relates to this case."

It took us about five minutes to finish stacking books, and then I stepped away to gently revive my very indulgent librarian. We waited for her to lock the library doors and then the two of us escorted her to a horse-drawn hackney.

Brian was patient enough to wait until they cantered away before extending his elbow with the words: "Now, Portia Adams, tell me your theories and why it matters that you understand dead bodies as well as our prime suspect does."

CHAPTER TWELVE

It wasn't until almost two weeks later, though, that I could finally test my theory with the real perpetrator. Flowers that had been shivering buds in April had burst into colorful bloom in May, and everyone seemed happier for it despite the increase in rain.

I waited and waited for another burglary, but the pattern seemed finally to be broken, as days went by without any new incidents reported. Perhaps the thief had finally sated his appetite, or perhaps he had moved on from London.

Every evening I bothered Brian Dawes with the same question, and every day I repeated the process with my professors: had anything else been reported stolen?

Finally, on a Friday in June, my prayers were answered, at the cost of someone else's fortune — another robbery.

Brian, good man that he was, came racing up my steps to deliver the news.

I answered his knock with a question even before fully opening the door. "Has something been stolen?" I demanded.

"Yes, miss. Trudy Bennett has reported a stolen necklace," he answered with a laugh. "*Now* will you tell me why you have been waiting for another incident? We had been hoping this spree was over, but you had the opposite hope."

I blushed, because it did seem somehow immoral to wait for someone else's bad fortune in order for me to prove a theory, but I honestly couldn't contain my excitement. "I will, but only if you arrest Ben Fawkes on Sunday morning, very first thing," I replied with a grin.

"Sunday morning?" he replied, understandably confused. "We all believe him to be the man, so if you have new evidence, let us go and arrest him right now, before he has a chance to sell the spoils from his newest heist."

I shook my head determinedly as he came into the room, stepping carefully around the papers and plates. "I promise you, if I am right, the latest stolen goods are quite safe until Sunday morning. Will you be reprimanded for arresting him, though?"

"This is about the theory you came up with at Guy's Hospital, isn't it?" he said, waggling a finger at me.

I nodded as he crouched down beside me and we fleshed out a quick plan right then and there for how to best drop the net and avoid risking Brian's career. I appreciated again how open he was to my opinion despite my untried hand in this field, looking up at him as he stroked his strong jaw, thinking hard about the details I was describing.

"What?" he asked as I paused mid-explanation.

"Why do you believe me?" I asked, truly curious as to his answer. "Why do you take my opinion so seriously? It is one that is so amateur when compared to the insights around you every day."

He moved to a kneeling position, his elbows on his thighs, his brow furrowed, "Well, I suppose because you are so adamant in your beliefs at so young an age, and because I've seen how quickly your mind works. Also, you think ... I don't know, differently from anyone at the Yard these days, and I think we need more of that."

I blushed at his kind words.

"And of course, there is your very heritage," he said, looking round at the room. "I am willing to make a great leap for the granddaughter of such a prolific detective and man."

I lowered my eyes, unwilling to let him see the tears that threatened to appear at his final statement — it was so much the destiny I was hoping for.

We had just settled the details when my guardian arrived. Brian made his polite goodbyes and winked at me on his way out — the plan was on!

The thrill of this chase must have shown on my face as Mrs. Jones finished removing her shawl. As she gracefully pulled off her kid gloves I noticed that she had removed her beautiful new ring with the turquoise stones and replaced it with an older band.

A prickle of unease ran down my spine, though at the time I wasn't entirely sure of the cause.

"You look better," she remarked, settling into her favorite chair beside the fireplace where Brian and I had so recently been planning.

"Yes, I am, thank you, and you?" I said, my excitement at the case fading, replaced by a new unease I could not explain.

"Oh, age has its benefits to be sure, but I confess I am starting to feel its ill effects as well," she said.

Worriedly, I took a good look at her now and could not perceive any difference in complexion, and I said so.

"Oh, sometimes, Portia, you will find as you get older that it is the restlessness of the soul that drives you, not the body. Quite the opposite of youth." She sighed dramatically.

I asked whether there was anything I could do to aid with such a problem and she laughed in response, a girlish, tinkling sound. "Oh heavens, no, my dear, and don't worry yourself. This malaise is most easily solved."

She shifted in her chair, her eyes taking on a dreamy sheen. "I think it is time I took my ease at one of my more rural homes, away from the hustle and bustle of London."

Since the busy streets of a large city were one of her purported loves, I filed that statement away without comment and merely nodded. "Where?"

"Perhaps Lyon, I have a lovely apartment there I haven't been in for years. Or maybe even Cairo."

"You have a home in Cairo?" I burst out, unable to contain my surprise at so exciting a destination.

"I have an arrangement with a friend there, yes," she answered with a smile. "Would you like to join me?"

"Very much so!" I said, eyes wide as she described the exotic foods and culture in detail.

"The *kofta*, oh there is this little street of vendors in the east end of Cairo." She shook her head with a smile, taking my hand. "It is indescribably good, my girl, and you would never know about it unless you were with someone who had found it before.

"The very streets smell like cinnamon, and from the moment you arrive the smells of spice and sugar just seem to envelope you."

She closed her eyes in remembrance. "Even weeks after getting home, all I need to is pick up something I wore there and smell it, and it takes me right back. So too will your very being become infused with the aromas of the East."

We talked late into the night, planning a fantastic tour in the fall, when the heat would be less of an issue.

By the time Mrs. Jones left, my mind was whirling with images of camels and pyramids and I fell asleep marveling at the tragic circumstances of losing my mother and my home that had brought me such an opportunity.

Sleep, though, brought dreams of a very different nature, filled with jewels and Turkish silks and the splashing of water.

CHAPTER THIRTEEN

I woke late in the morning that Saturday, puzzling over the dream. Despite having a grand plan with Brian to execute the following day, I found myself instead distracted by the confusing elements of the dream.

My morning walk was disturbed by this confusion as I made my way to my customary café. About halfway along my trek, I noticed someone was following me — which was also odd since I had been so absorbed in my thoughts.

The man was obviously not really trying to disguise his pursuit, so I kept him in my sights as I turned corners and finally made it to the small café.

I took a seat outside, facing in the direction I had come from, and the waiter came to take my usual Saturday order. I was therefore not in the least surprised when the gentleman who had been following me took the seat across from me.

I felt no danger radiating from his large frame. I guessed his age at over seventy. He was obviously of African descent, over two hundred pounds, and revealed a shiny bald head when he removed his hat.

"Good morning, young miss," he said finally, enduring my silent scrutiny with an equally assessing eye. His accent was pure British, from Liverpool if I had to guess.

"Good morning," I replied respectfully, nodding once again at my waiter as he dropped off my coffee.

"For you, sir?" the waiter asked, a hint of confusion in his voice.

"Tea," he replied, barely glancing up at the waiter but placing double the bill in notes on the table.

The waiter fairly sprinted off to get the tea.

I took a sip of my coffee before deciding to approach this conversation head on. "You have been following me, sir, for some distance, and I can see that exercise is something you do often with your physique at such an advanced age. So I would not keep you — what can I do for you?"

He looked surprised by my observations, as most people did when they first met me. "Advanced age, eh? She was right, you are pert."

"Indeed? And who is *she*?" I demanded, putting down my cup to glare at the man.

The waiter returned with a pot of tea and a cup, whisking it onto the table and scooping up his payment with a grin.

The old man's clothing consisted of a worn pair of knickerbockers and a loose sweater, and looking from the twists and turns of his nose and down at his knuckles, I quickly surmised why.

I leaned forward as the older gentleman tipped the pot toward his cup. "Are you by chance the type of man who has an interest in accosting young women?" I said, hoping to shock him into the truth.

"Ha!" he said with a laugh, shaking his large head as he took a sip of tea. "Not in the way you mean, though." He leaned forward, forcing me to back up. "If I were that type of man, you didn't make it hard to follow you at all."

"Who are you?" I demanded, my annoyance growing.

"Also, if I were that type of man, you can't tell me that's how you would deal with me!" he said, shaking his head with a smile.

I crossed my arms, glaring at him.

"The name's Jenkins, Asher Jenkins, and I'm someone who's gonna help you," he declared, clapping his hands. "I promised your guardian I'd teach you how to take care of yourself, and by God, that's what I'm gonna do."

I rolled my eyes. "Are you ... you're a friend of Mrs. Jones?" I demanded. "Why didn't you say so right away?"

He shrugged his massive shoulders. "I wanted to see what you were about first. Get a feelin' for what I'm dealin' with."

My shoulders came up defensively as he took another casual sip of tea, glaring at another customer who seemed too interested in our discussion. "And?"

"Eh?" he replied, swinging his gaze back my way.

I blew out my breath. "And what do you see? What are you dealing with?"

He looked me up and down. "A soft American who's totally out of her element and thinks she can wander all over London like she owns the place. That's what I see. But don't you worry your head, little Miss Adams, I made a promise to Irene."

"To do what? Teach me how to box?" I challenged. "To muscle my way out of trouble?"

He spat out his tea, causing even more of the café's patrons to glance over and then quickly glance away.

"You're a boxer, possibly a professional one based on the number of times your nose has been broken and reset," I said as he pulled a hanky from his pocket to clean his face. "I can't believe you'd still be practicing that sport at your, yes, advanced age, so you've graduated into what? Professional intimidation?"

"I call it trainin', little miss," he replied, pulling the hanky away from a lopsided grin and making me add a broken jaw to his list of very old injuries.

"Well, I am not interested in being trained, Mr. Jenkins," I said, standing and looking him in the eye. "Thank you for your interest, but I shall relay that message to my guardian myself. Good day."

He laughed, a great bellowing sound that seemed to come from his very shoes. "Oh you do that. I only wish I was there to see you relay..." he guffawed again, "...that message."

I stalked off, the sound of his laughter following me all the way down the block.

* * *

It only took three hours of research at the Bodleian Library at Oxford to find newspaper articles crowing about the great boxer Asher "Bruiser" Jenkins. He had been quite a prizefighter in his day, but had disappeared in the press after 1895. Jenkins had been arrested twice in the 1890s on charges of theft, but only one of those had gone to trial, resulting in a three-year jail term he had served at Wandsworth prison.

I sat back in my chair, stretching my sore muscles as I considered his connection to my guardian. They seemed to be from opposite ends of the social spectrum — how would they even have met? Finding no comfort in stretches, I stood, pacing around the oak table I had piled high with newsprint and anthologies of newspapers, taking a deep breath to enjoy the soothing smells of old books and paper. I had spent much of my free time in the Queen and Lisgar Branch Library in Toronto, where my mother had been a part-time librarian and where I had hoped to become a page someday. With effort, I shook my head free of the memories that would derail my current endeavor, glancing at the stately window to my left.

The sun was setting, and I knew the librarians would want to close up soon, so with a sigh I picked up a few of the larger bound anthologies and walked them back over to the shelves I had found them on. I went back to my table, collecting up the newspapers and stacking them more neatly. These would need to be re-filed by the library staff.

How did Bruiser Jenkins know Mrs. Jones? More importantly, how had she come to trust him enough to send him my way? What did they have in common?

I suddenly thought back to the dream I had about the sound of splashing and the jewels that had been stolen, and remembered that had been on the night Mrs. Jones dropped by with the silks and jewelry from some exotic locale. A locale she had been very cagey about.

"A locale where maybe a Turkish millionaire could buy a stolen tiara?" I whispered.

CHAPTER FOURTEEN

Early in the morning on Sunday, before the sun had even made its appearance, Constable Dawes made his arrest.

Into Scotland Yard was bustled a disheveled and sleepy Ben Fawkes. I waited at the Yard for the two men to arrive, and to witness Fawkes's attitude — no longer grinning and at ease, but angry and squirming to get away.

Brian and I had conspired to keep Fawkes in the Yard for as long as we could, so Dawes took his time with paperwork and questions, asking basic things over and over again until Fawkes was nearly pulling out his hair in frustration. I knew Brian would have to release him soon, so, giving him a nod, I proceeded to the next part of our plan.

With not a little effort, I had convinced my professor and two of his best men to accompany me down to a spot I had previously scouted out on the east side of Westminster Bridge. Archer was only persuaded when I finally told him about chasing down the eyewitness he had hidden from me — and even then, I could tell he was just humoring me with this effort. I also knew that this was my one chance to prove myself with this case. It had to work!

"I cannot imagine what Sergeant Michaels is going to say when he hears about this," my professor whispered to me as we crouched behind some crates we had strategically arranged.

"Sir, how much longer will we be here?" whispered one of the officers, his tiny mustache wiggling as he spoke. It was obviously itchy — was he new to growing facial hair?

I shook my head, fighting off the distraction of a new puzzle. "If I am right, Professor, Officers, Sergeant Michaels will soon have one less case on his desk."

"How do we even know he will come this way, though?" the other officer muttered. "He could take any of the bridges to get across the water, and his home is not even on this side of the river!"

"Because he will be coming from the Yard, and this is his destination," I explained again, growing annoyed with these men. We had only been waiting fifteen minutes, for goodness sake! I acknowledged inwardly that part of my annoyance was actually worry I was wrong about this theory, but before I could follow that depressing path of doubt further, the man we had all been waiting for made an appearance.

Across the bridge, walking at a very quick pace and turning around every few minutes to see if he was being followed, was Mr. Fawkes. Obviously, Brian had run out of excuses and had released him.

"What the hell?" whispered one of the officers, also recognizing him.

"Now, remember, don't move until I say!" I warned the men as two of them tensed to leap out despite my earlier remonstrations.

Meanwhile, Fawkes had gained the bridge and was suspiciously glancing this way and that. He stood there turning in a circle, looking down the river and up, until he finally seemed satisfied that he was alone.

He reached over the side to grab a pole with a hook on the end the size of a man's fist — used by fishermen and others to scoop up items that fell into the water — and leaned over the side. He fished with it for a few minutes and then triumphantly hauled up a sack that we had previously observed floating amongst the general garbage and flotsam.

"Now!" I whispered excitedly as he got the sack in his hand and made to replace the hook.

Whistle signals rang out from my group.

"Halt!" yelled the officers in my cadre, quickly rushing out onto the bridge, to be joined by their fellows who had been hiding on the other side, alerted by the whistles.

Within moments, Fawkes was once again in police custody, and even angrier than he had been early this morning.

"'Ere! What's this?" he demanded as the sack was wrested from his hands.

I quickly covered my mouth and nose with my kerchief as one of the officers opened the bag. "Good God!" he exclaimed, nearly dropping the bag in shock at the stench.

I had wrapped some cloves and a stick of cinnamon into my kerchief in preparation for this moment, but I could still detect the rotten stink of death emanating from the dripping sack. There was yelling, and when I looked up, Sergeant Michaels making his way in the early morning light, followed by a defeated-looking Constable Brian Dawes. I hoped he had not gotten a tongue-lashing for his part in the morning's work.

"What the hell is going on here?" yelled Sergeant Michaels, huffing his way into our midst, where he cursed at the smell and pointed at the bag. "And what godawful thing is that you've dredged up from the river?"

Meanwhile, the officer had gotten over his initial shock and reached into the bag to pull out a necklace of sparkling emeralds covered in gore, blood and matted fur.

After a full moment of stunned silence, Constable Dawes recovered enough to say, "Miss. Bennett's emerald necklace!"
Everyone started talking at once, none more volubly than the unfortunate Fawkes, who was protesting his innocence at the top of his lungs. Several officers had stepped around to shake my hand, promising that they had never doubted me, and my professor was fairly glowing with pride at the compliments flowing all around.

"Enough!" barked Sergeant Michaels. "You two, take Fawkes back to the Yard immediately!"

The two officers holding Fawkes by the arms scampered away, one winking at me, the other tipping his hat deferentially.

"And you — what else is in that bag?" he demanded of the officer holding the bag and necklace.

"I believe it is a dead rat, sir," he answered, confused and looking to me for an explanation.

"Well, for heaven's sake, close that bag back up and get everything back to the station for evidence," Michaels ordered. "And clean that bauble thoroughly before you call on Miss Bennett!"

Constable Brian Dawes was grinning from ear to ear, and I couldn't help but return the expression — an action that drew the attention of the sergeant and my professor.

"You two," Michaels said, pointing to each of us in turn, "start talking."

Brian just shook his head and gestured at me, but my professor broke in. "Yes, Miss Adams, your theory has surely been proven, but how *did* you know?"

I took a breath. "It was the smell, you see. That is what made everything clear to me finally."

"Made *what* clear?" interrupted Sergeant Michaels, flapping his arms dramatically.

But my good professor simply raised his hand to let me continue.

"You had your man, Sergeant Michaels, you knew who was responsible. What you didn't know was why he was never caught red-handed," I explained, pacing as I spoke. "That first day, when you brought Mr. Fawkes in for questioning, Madame LaPointe was unable to make a positive identification, but she remembered a smell."

Michaels looked surprised again. "How could you know that? I never wrote that in the report — it wasn't a useful piece of evidence. The man worked as an assistant undertaker, of course he smelled bad!"

"Except he didn't always smell bad," I pointed out. "The first time he was brought into the police station, Fawkes smelled normal. It was on a separate and, I thought, random run-in, that I too noticed what Madame LaPointe had noticed — that horrible rotting smell."

I halted and gestured in the direction the bag had been taken back to the Yard as evidence. "Both times the smell was noticed, Fawkes was holding a large sack. It seems fair to postulate that the sack was the origin of the smell, not Fawkes himself. But then there was the size of the sack. If you were planning to steal single pieces of jewelry at each robbery, why carry such a large bag? Madame LaPointe said the sack was full when he was escaping her rooms. Well, what was it full of to give off that smell? The tiara was the only thing reported stolen that night, so what else was in this sack?"

I looked at the three of them, and only Dawes shrugged. But Michaels sputtered, "Wait, I don't care about the size of the bag *or* the cursed smell. Are you saying that Fawkes would run past this bridge and throw his loot over the side! Are all the other jewels at the bottom of this river too? What manner of plan is that?"

I continued as if I hadn't heard him. "At first I couldn't place the smell, but by chance I recognized it when I was near a butcher's stall in the Smithfield Market. The smell was that of a decomposing body. Then, it was just a matter of understanding why Fawkes stuffed the dead body of an animal in a sack with the jewels he had just stolen."

"To dissuade anyone who found the bag from opening it?" my professor offered.

"Maybe," I answered, "but the night that Fawkes was caught, you had a half dozen officers down here searching for Madame LaPointe's tiara. Your men wouldn't have been dissuaded from searching a sack just because it smelled bad, would they, Sergeant?"

"Certainly not," he said stiffly.

"In addition, as you said, his modus operandi was to fling his stolen goods into the river as he ran past," I said, my fists bunching, "and that's where his knowledge of dead bodies was useful to him."

I resumed pacing. "Fawkes knows that when a body first becomes a corpse, it is heavy, and the smell is there, but it gets worse as the body decays. He also knows that within twelve hours rigor mortis sets in."

"Yes, yes, but then why throw a sack full of jewels and a dead rat that would weigh the bag down to the bottom of the river?" snapped the sergeant impatiently.

"Because in another twelve hours, the gases build up in the body," I explained. "It's called bloat, and it would have caused the sack, which had initially sunk to the bottom of the river, to float, buoyed by the trapped gases."

"Incredible," said Constable Dawes.

"Impossible," said Sergeant Michaels.

"Elementary," said my professor with a grin.
"I promise you, that is the second stage of decomposition. I researched the phenomenon thoroughly last week," I insisted. "Fawkes knew this from his work, and used this to his advantage to carry out his crimes."

"I was there, sir," Brian put forth, his eyes sparkling. "The images were disgusting, but Miss Adams had textbook after textbook describing the progress of decomposition."

"And you knew that twenty-four hours after the robbery, Fawkes would come down here desperately seeking his now floating bag," summarized my professor with pride.

I nodded. "Indeed. Throwing the bag into the river, Dawes knew that he always had a twenty-four-hour window to lay low or even be arrested. With his latest robbery on Friday, his twenty-four hours were up this very morning. The third stage of decomposition is heralded by the pressures of the gases finally escaping the body, often in violent ways. At which point the sack would eventually sink, to be lost to Fawkes forever."

Sergeant Michaels finally found his voice again. "And you surmised all of this?"

"Extensive research and simple induction, sir," I answered, hoping I didn't sound arrogant, but unable to suppress the smile on my lips.

He snapped his mouth shut, looking as if he wanted to say more. Instead, he just bowed slightly at the waist and, barking at Dawes to follow him, headed back at a quick pace toward the Yard.

With a wink, my professor extended his elbow and we followed them back across Westminster Bridge.

CHAPTER FIFTEEN

The press made much of the case, but I asked for, and was granted, anonymity for my involvement. Indeed, Sergeant Michaels was quite happy to take credit for my work, but publicly, and at Scotland Yard, he shared credit for the capture with Constable Dawes, so I was well satisfied.

In addition, the reward offered by Miss Bennett for the return of her emerald necklace was personally delivered to me by the most appreciative lady.

It wasn't until almost the end of June that my guardian showed up again.

"Well, you *have* been busy," she remarked as I ushered her into my apartments. She handed me her shawl. "I asked dear Mrs. Dawes to bring us up a spot of tea."

"Have I?" I answered, only slightly amused.

She glanced at me, perhaps assessing my mood before she answered. Finding it jovial rather than sarcastic, she said, "Come, come, you have solved your first case — surely this is a moment to celebrate?"

Mrs. Dawes trundled in with a precariously balanced serving tray. I quickly relieved her of it.

"The 'moment', as you put it, was almost two weeks ago, Mrs. Jones," I corrected respectfully, pouring us each a cup of tea as Mrs. Dawes exited the room.

"Oh pish tosh!" Mrs. Jones said with a wave of her hand. "I've been abroad, and your professor Archer's glowing letters took time to reach me in Lyon. I came as soon as I could. I was taking the baths, my dear, relieving my old ailments."

"Mmm," I murmured, taking a sip of my tea as I regarded her.

We sat in quiet assessment of each other for a few minutes, until I finally had to put down my cup with a sigh. "It will not do, madam. We must discuss Bruiser Jenkins."

She said nothing for a beat and then, "Ah, I was wondering if sending him your way was a mistake."

I nodded. "Of course it was, Mrs. Jones — sending a former thief to train me in ... I don't even know what — what could you be thinking?"

"Of your safety, my dear girl," she replied, putting down her cup.

"So you sent a former boxer, a criminal who has spent time in jail, to protect me?" I demanded.

She waved her hands and my gaze hardened, unwilling to be pushed off the subject this time.

"That little escapade on the bridge scared me, and rightfully so!" she said, her eyes flashing. "You cannot be putting yourself in danger like that — you are a young impressionable girl! You are not Watson or Holmes!

"No, I am not, madam," I said coldly, "but even I noticed the ring you wore a few weeks ago that is now so obviously missing from your finger."
She threw up her hands. "I knew you made the connection — curse your bloodline! When did you know?"

"Not positively, until just now when you claimed to be taking the baths at Lyon," I admitted. "If you were spending all your time in the baths, either your rings would be spotless and shiny or the skin on your fingers would be chafed from taking them on and off. They are neither — therefore you were not at the baths. You were avoiding me in London because you knew I was close to solving the case."

She sighed again but didn't disagree.

"You sent Bruiser Jenkins to me because you are old friends," I said, daring her to disagree. "Because you too have walked on the wrong side of the law. It is the only way you would trust me, whom you purport to love, into the care of a muscle-bound criminal."

She opened her mouth and then closed it abruptly.

"You sold Madame LaPointe's tiara to a Turkish millionaire and returned with a Turkish ring and Turkish silks," I listed. "Turkish jewelry often has combinations of two metals, a local trait, and the stones — turquoise — are well known to the region."

"What do you intend to do with this idea, Portia?" she asked, raising an eyebrow, neither denying nor admitting anything.

I didn't tell her how close I had come to turning her in. How the looks of appreciation from Brian and his contemporaries had been as addictive an idea as my pursuance of my grandfather's work. What if I could also give them the ringleader? What a coup that would be! Professionally, at least.

My guardian lived on the wrong side of the law. I would guess that she had for decades before my existence. But to lose her to the penal system, as surely could have been arranged, would have taken away one of my last connections to my mother, small as it was. This was a woman who had known my grandmother and my grandfather. Who had agreed to support me and had so far done exactly as she had promised. And I had to admit that she had become important to me, not as a replacement for my mother, but as a member of my new, less formalized family here in London. I did love this woman. I did need her.

And to lose her would have taken away my first connection to this, my new life.

I could only hope that if the truth ever came out about her real involvement in this case, she would be far away from London, and that I could continue to look Brian Dawes in the eye.

"I won't even bother to ask if you still have any of the items you conspired to steal. You would have rid yourself of them as soon as you could, probably in another country like you did with the tiara," I said, getting no reaction from her, but expecting none.

"You knew which jewelry to take, and you told Fawkes of it, and of the most opportune times to steal the items. You knew when the owners would be out of the house because you ran in the same circles," I said. "So my question is this: why has Fawkes not named you as his client?"

She shrugged, but I could tell she had an answer, and I was determined to have it.

"Oh, very well then. We never actually spoke, we corresponded through telegram only," she finally admitted. "He has no idea who gave him the information or paid him for his work. Are you content now?"

"I cannot condone your actions, Mrs. Jones," I replied, caressing my teacup with my forefinger as I spoke, "but if you can promise me, here and now, that you will halt all criminal activity, then I am willing to move past this."

She looked down at her lap before answering. "And if I cannot make that promise?"

I leaned forward to project my determination better. "Then we are finished. I will thank you for your support, and I will ask for your last act as guardian to be to remove yourself legally from my life, even as I ask you to remove yourself physically from my flat."

Her lower lip trembled and I fought down my own emotional reaction. The words were not easy to say, but actually doing what I had harshly laid out was even worse to imagine.

"Will you take the help from Jenkins?" she asked softly. "He is a teddy bear, I swear to you, Portia. He is a sweet man who happens to have the skills to train you to take care of yourself. You don't know how much you frightened me. I don't want to be frightened like that again. Please."

I could see just how much this meant to her and felt any residual anger seep away, to be replaced by an appreciation that someone cared so much about me. "If you trust him so much, then yes, I suppose I could compromise with you on training with him. If only to alleviate your worry."

She nodded, and her voice rough with sorrow, she said, "Then I promise." She reached her hand across to mine. "I promise. Do you believe me?"

"Yes," I said, sitting back and closing my eyes with a satisfied sigh.

"That I remember," she remarked, smiling again finally. I opened my eyes.

"The end of a case in this apartment was marked by the solution of the puzzle, not the arrest of the perpetrator. By and large that fell to the rather obtuse Inspector Lestrade," she explained.

"And for my grandfather?" I asked, curious.

"Watson was always of two minds. Part of him thrilled at his friend's success once again, and another part worried about the interim between cases," she said, tilting her head. "Is that something I should worry about with you?"

I thought about it for a minute, and then a sparkle came into my eye, thinking of a way that we could together repay the victims in this case for their losses.

I leaned forward. "Oh, my dear Mrs. Jones, there is *always* another case."

She laughed, wiping the last of her tears from her eyes. "Tell me about it, then, my dear Portia. I am all ears."

CHAPTER SIXTEEN

We should pick a regular night, don't you think?" Brian said, calling my attention back to him. We were shelling peas in his mother's kitchen later that same day, and I had fallen into the repetitive rhythm of the work.

"I'm sorry, what?"

Leek soup simmered on the stove behind us as we sat at the small wooden table, the smell thick and inviting.

Mrs. Dawes popped her head into the kitchen. "I'm stepping over to the O'Reilly's to borrow an egg," she said, pulling on her jacket, "an' your father is still out walkin' the dogs."

"I mean for you to come to dinner, here, with us," Brian explained as soon as his mother was gone. "You know, make it a regular night."

I couldn't help but smile. "That would be nice, and probably more efficient for your mother than dropping in randomly so that she doesn't know if she's cooking for three or four. I'm sure that's annoying."

He snorted, his dimples making a brief appearance. "My mother is far too intimidated by your Mrs. Jones to worry about efficiencies — I think she'd be fine with you coming down every night if it meant Mrs. Jones would show her rare approval."

I glanced up at him from my hands, dying to ask how he'd feel about that, but too cowardly to actually do it.

"She hasn't been around for a few weeks. Your guardian, I mean," Brian continued, picking up his bowl to fish out a pea that was slightly off-color. "Until I saw her today, I thought maybe she had decided to leave you to your own devices. That wouldn't be so bad, would it? To not have a guardian at all?"
I cocked my head. "You don't like Mrs. Jones much, do you?"

He shrugged. "It's not that I don't like her. She doesn't much seem to like me," he said, raising his brown eyes to meet mine. "As soon as she sees me her shoulders come up an' so, might I say, does her nose..."

I laughed but inwardly agreed with his astute observations, though I now knew her reaction to be one of a decades-old adversary.

"I have to admit, I have come to care for and even admire Mrs. Jones," I said instead, the peas in my hands falling agreeably into my bowl, "though she has her foibles, as we all do."

"I like how she treats you," he replied, pausing in his shelling to speak. "She cares for you very much, and I like that you have that in your life."

I didn't know what to say about that, but I felt warmth in my belly at his concern for me.

"Well, also, she's the only connection I have to Dr. Watson and my grandmother. Even if she weren't my guardian, I'd still want a relationship with her," I stammered, forcing my words to slow. "She is, after all, the only person who can tell me about that entire side of my family. Though getting information out of her is not an easy task."

I popped out three peas at the same time, two of them flying in opposite directions, and only one actually landing in my bowl.

"Well ... not the only person," Brian said.

I looked at him quizzically, locating one of the peas that had rolled under my chair and straightening with it in hand.

"There is, after all, Sherlock Holmes," he said with a smile.

A case of darkness: Casebook 2

London, Fall 1930

The ever-deepening financial woes of the world continued as summer turned to fall at 221 Baker Street. The class sizes for this semester at my college dropped by two thirds as the less affluent ladies were unable to find the required tuition to continue studying. So far, Britain had fared better than the colonies as the economic depression took hold, but that only meant that the breadlines on this side of the ocean were shorter, not that they didn't exist. This also meant that the financial support for the education of women, only starting to build momentum, suffered more than the education of their male peers. Less funding for the college meant less scholarships and grants, which all led to fewer students.

With smaller class sizes came more scrutiny and, very quickly, the suggestion was made to cancel some classes and combine others. One of the more contentious suggestions was that a few of our classes be combined with that of the corresponding men's college so both schools could save some money in the worrying financial climate.

There were of course protests on both sides, but eventually a deal was struck whereby our lecture on tort law was relocated to the boy's college.

Suffice to say that of the already small classes of girls left to study that fall, even fewer were willing to brave the heckling and general awkwardness found in a mixed classroom. But despite this (or rather because of it, according to Brian) I relished that class above all others.

It gave me insight into a breed of men I seldom had access to. I would never complain about my life before London, but I had grown up in a working-class family in Canada. My mother worked constantly, sometimes as a librarian, other times supplementing that meager salary by caring for neighborhood children. I hadn't known at the time, but the various tutors I had had over the years had been paid for not by my mother, but now suspected they were paid for by Dr. Watson. The few men I had known in that time were the drunken friends of my ex-stepfather, the type of man I felt I had a depressingly clear sense of.

The men in my tort class were literally a different stock of human. I took careful notes on all, knowing that one of the keys of investigative work was observation and gathering of data. Someday, this knowledge could very well help me solve a crime. I had no idea that I would get the opportunity to use that information so soon.

"So, how goes the battle, little miss?" Mrs. Dawes huffed at me one night as I struggled in the front door with an unaccommodating umbrella.

"Oh," I replied, finally bringing the misshapen device under control, "not too badly, thank you."

Since this was usually the extent of our parley, I was surprised to see her still standing there after I had worked off my soaked overcoat. She was shifting from foot to foot nervously, so I enquired if anything were amiss.

"I may have," she stammered out, "that is ... I did ... perhaps ... let a young man into your rooms a few minutes ago."

"I'm sorry?" I answered, eyebrows raised as I glanced up the stairs to my flat. "What man?"

"He seemed quite nice, most attractive indeed," she hedged, now adding wringing of her hands to the movement of her feet. "But after he convinced me to let him wait upstairs for you, it occurred to me that it, well, it might not be quite proper..."

I considered my words carefully despite my growing annoyance. "Indeed, and perhaps even dangerous, Mrs. Dawes?" I said, picking up my umbrella and for the first time wishing I hadn't delayed my first training session with Jenkins. "Tell me, is your son home?"

"Brian? Oh, yes, he is. Shall I get him?" she replied, confused.

"Could you, please?" I asked, maintaining my calm with effort. I looked around the area for a coat that might give me a clue as to who was sitting in my apartment, but saw nothing I didn't recognize. No strange footsteps scuffed my stairs, but Mrs. Dawes was meticulous in her cleaning habits, so I rarely found a clue there anyway.

Brian was duly fetched, and after being apprised of the situation he took a moment to reprimand his mother for allowing strangers into the apartment. He had his sleeves rolled up to the elbows and suds still clung to the hair on his arms, indicating that he had been washing dishes when called out.

"Miss Adams is, after all, a single woman," he said to his mother, his hand on her shoulder to soften his remonstration. He glanced up at me, his eyes running over me appreciatively. "Though an entirely capable woman, of course..."

I tried to speak and found that I could still feel the heat of his gaze upon me, so instead I pointed up the stairs with my umbrella. He nodded, patted his mother on the arm, and then led the way up the stairs.

Opening the door wide, we took a good look inside. The room looked as it always did — papers everywhere, plates and cups stacked neatly near the door — but with a new addition: a man sitting comfortably in one of my wingback chairs. A man I instantly recognized.

"Mr. Barclay, isn't it?" I asked, stepping into my home and lowering my umbrella.

"Yes!" he replied, springing to his feet and bowing slightly. He extended his hand to Brian. "And you are, sir?"

The fashionable suit Barclay wore was finely tailored and freshly pressed, showing only one line of demarcation over his left leg. His shoes were polished and black, his hair fashionably styled, and cologne wafted out of his collar as he stepped closer to us. He was handsome in a way that I knew pleased many of the girls, with wide-set green eyes, long, dark eyelashes, high cheekbones and a perfect smile you could have easily found on a film set.

"Constable Brian Dawes," said my companion with a curt nod, and then looking at me with an uneasy glance. "Do you know this man, then, Miss Adams?"

"I do," I affirmed. "Mr. Barclay is a classmate of mine, possibly stopping here on his way home from rehearsals." I laid my hand on Brian's arm, feeling it tense and then relax slowly under my fingers. "Thank you so much for making sure all was well, Constable."

Brian took his cue, giving Barclay another once-over before giving me a furtive glance and retreating down the stairs, leaving the door pointedly open.

"However did you know I was on my way home from rehearsals, Miss Adams?" Mr. Barclay said wonderingly as I took a better look around my apartment.

"The cross-wise mark across your left trouser leg. A sword recently hung there, though not a heavy one by the look of how lightly it pressed against you," I answered automatically. "As I know, you are studying law and are not in the military, and since it was lighter than a real sword, I suspect that it was a prop. And where else would you need a prop but in a play?"

He gaped at that, so I continued. "As delighted as I am to see you, sir, I confess I do not recall that we had made an appointment to meet, let alone that I had invited you into my home."

He blushed at the frost in my tone and held out his hands apologetically. "My dear Miss Adams, I am terribly embarrassed by my own lack of manners. If you wish for me to leave, you have but to say the word and I will do so immediately."

He picked up his hat and gloves as he spoke to prove the truth of his words, but my curiosity overcame my annoyance, so I said, "As long as it does not happen again, sir, we can consider how you arrived here of no consequence, and proceed to the why."

Mr. Barclay's face broke into a charming grin, and he turned toward my fireplace. I took a seat. We heard Mrs. Dawes struggling up the stairs with a tray. Barclay gallantly took the platter of biscuits and tea in china cups with small blue flowers decorating their stems from her with many thanks that left her blushing and giggling her way back down the stairs. I poured each of us a generous helping of tea as he took a seat across from me, waving off my offer of sugar or milk.

"It is most imposing to actually be in this room, don't you think?" he said finally, picking up his cup. "I wonder that you manage to live here surrounded by so much history."

I shrugged, having spent months becoming acclimatized to my remarkable circumstances. "It becomes easier as time passes, I assure you."

He took a gulp of tea. "And the stories being told about you at the college are true, then? That you helped the police capture the thief, Fawkes?"

He said the last with such a hopeful turn that I took pity on him and started the conversation he so obviously did not want to. "I did, and if it is help you need, I would be more than happy to bring Constable Dawes back upstairs to take on your case. I am sure he would—"

But Barclay was shaking his head, so I stopped mid-sentence. "No, no, that will not do. This sort of case ... it is so very sensitive." He stood up and began pacing in agitation, cup in hand.

"Involving the police would bring too much attention to it, and if it were mishandled, or if the press were to find out, the damage to my family would be..."

"Then I am not sure what I can do for you, sir," I said, spreading my hands. "Despite the history of this room and my actions this summer, I am not a private detective, and investigation is at present a hobby to me, not a profession."

"Yes, but that is exactly what I need," he said excitedly, "a secret detective! Someone who does not seek fame and glory but has the skills to get the job done, and who, at the resolution of the investigation, will not air our private issues to the public, all of which you have proven to be very capable of."

I considered his words, hiding my excitement. It was true that I had followed more than a few crimes in the papers since the summer, but nothing dramatic — no unsolved mysteries to really sink my teeth into. And I missed the thrill of that chase; there really was no feeling like it.

"At least let me tell you my tale," he begged, handsome features turning into a most earnest plea, "and then make your decision? I will abide no matter what you decide."

I nodded and settled back to listen as he took a deep breath.

"My father is the Right Honourable Judge Marcus Barclay of the Superior Courts. A remarkable man, Miss Adams. I only wish you could have met him at the height of his judicial career. He was a force to be reckoned with, inside and outside the courtroom, I must admit. He has been forced to retire this past spring due to an illness that forbids him from stressful work, as of course trying criminal cases at his level must be.

"He was struck ill quite suddenly, and has, over the past months, lost many of his basic abilities. We fear the worst, but doctor after doctor has been consulted, all giving us the same maddening answer: nothing can be found to be physically wrong with the man."

My mother's own misdiagnosis and fatal illness were still very much in my mind, so I felt this man's pain keenly.

"Understandably, the whole family has been affected," he continued after a sip, "and by whole family, I actually exaggerate, since there are only the two of us left: my elder sister and myself, our good mother having passed when we were but small children."

I poured us each another cup of tea and he took the refilled cup with thanks. "My sister has ... changed," he said hesitantly, searching for the right words, "and it is more than worry over my father. She has changed so drastically from the girl I knew that I know there is something more behind it. That is why I am here. I want you to discover the true cause of my sister's woes and help me to remove them."

"I don't think I understand," I said.

"Up until my father's illness, my sister was the most agreeable lady you could ever meet," Barclay said. "She was the finest of young women, engaged to a gentleman of the highest standard. But when my father sickened, something changed in her. She became withdrawn and suspicious, she stopped going out socially, she stopped attending college, and then she abruptly ended her engagement to Mr. Ridley. She seems obsessed with our father's illness to the point that she rarely leaves his side."

I nodded sympathetically. "It sounds to me like she is understandably depressed by the prospect of losing her parent, more so than is healthy, I admit, but certainly not surprising. Is she especially close to your father?"

"Elaine and my father have always been very, very close," Barclay admitted, "more so than Elaine and I or my father and I, that I will acknowledge. But I have considered that, and I truly believe that is not all there is to her passion."

"Having lost my own dear mother recently, I understand that single-minded focus of trying to help save the ones you love," I said. "Have the doctors talked to her about your father?"

He shook his head. "At first, but her questions turned to harassment when nothing could be discovered. It has progressed to the point that she has barred anyone, doctors, friends, servants, even myself, from entering his rooms. She sleeps in his anteroom — she moved her bed in there two months ago — and the only times I am permitted to see him is while in her presence."

"What does your father think of this?" I asked.

"Initially, he thought the same as we did, and as you do, that she was distraught at how quickly his health was declining," Barclay said.

"But before he lost the power of speech a few months ago, he confided in me that he thought someone," he hesitated again, "someone might be threatening my sister. It would explain her paranoid turn."

I sat back. "That is a serious accusation, sir, and I again remind you of the constable living downstairs who would be most interested in this case. Has naught been done to ascertain if there is any evidence of that?"

"No, no!" he said miserably. "My sister refuses to talk about it, and as to my father's theories, I cannot confirm them and he can no longer explain. I have asked my sister again and again but have had no luck, and she refuses to speak to anyone, friend or family."

I steepled my fingers. "And what is it you think I could do, sir?"

"I believe that she would confide in you as a woman of her age and intelligence, and that you, with your skills for deduction, could take what little information she would be willing to give you and decipher it!" he said, leaning forward. "Please, Miss Adams, I am desperate. Help me while I have time to reverse this situation and regain my beloved sister!"

"Induction," I corrected automatically, considering the situation. Despite my misgivings, his entreaties did not fall upon deaf ears, and I found myself saying, "But if your sister has closed herself off socially and barely leaves your father's rooms, how do you propose I gain her confidence?"

"I had thought..." he offered, not meeting my eyes, "that you might pose as my fiancée, and thereby gain access to our home and to my sister."

Color flooded my cheeks. "Oh, I think not, sir."

"I believe I could carry it off, though," he said excitedly, the passion for the craft increasing the man's charm and making me blush even more. "As you so astutely surmised, I flatter myself as to my abilities as an actor, a true passion of mine. You might have heard that I have secured the lead in our college production of the Scottish play."

I did not know and admitted to it freely. "I'm surprised you find time for acting amongst our studies, but I—"

"I make the time. It is a personal passion of mine," he interrupted. "Only my mother understood and shared my love for the stage, but I am determined to use the talent that God gave me!"

For one brief second I allowed myself to imagine walking around on James Barclay's arm, being the envy of the women in our classes, impressing Mrs. Jones ... but shook it off with effort.

"Be that as it may, for such a scheme to work we would need to lie to your family, and possibly mine, since questions will arise. Therefore, I cannot agree to this approach," I said firmly.

He blushed for a second time in our interview. "I thought you might not take to that. I do have another idea: my sister has recently taken an ad out in the newspaper, without consulting with me, for a part-time caregiver to come by and read to my father in the evenings."

I nodded. "Much more agreeable, and more believable that a student would seek part-time employment to supplement the costs of college. I shall answer the ad tomorrow."

"Perfect!" he exclaimed, rising to shake my hand energetically. "I need only ask for your fee, and your utmost silence on this subject."

We quickly negotiated a reasonable sum for the next two weeks of investigative work and said our goodbyes.

CHAPTER TWO

Two days later I received word from Miss Elaine Barclay that I would be granted an interview, with directions to their address in Hackney.

Arriving promptly at five p.m., I was ushered into the red-brick Tudor-style house by a smartly dressed butler with a most disagreeable frowning countenance, possibly due to the gout he was likely suffering from, as evidenced by his leaning heavily on his left foot. After relieving me of my outerwear, he asked that I follow him up a wide, painted staircase past wood-paneled walls and Jacobean paintings to one of the many bedroom doors on the second floor, where he knocked thrice.

"Come in," said a voice from inside, and the butler opened the door inward for me. I stepped into the darkened interior, my eyes adjusting to the simple candlelight.

The door closed behind me as the same voice said, "Please come in, have a seat to your right."

I could make out the shadowy form of the speaker seated on a chaise lounge and did as she bade, taking the seat in front of her. My curiosity at her appearance must have been obvious, because she said, "Do forgive the drama of this interview, Miss Adams, or may I call you Portia?"

"Portia will be fine, Miss Barclay," I replied cordially. "And I hope it is not too impertinent to ask, but it is a beautiful sunny day outside. Why do you sit in here with the drapes closed and these few candles to provide a trifling of light?"

"Is it a beautiful day?" she asked wistfully, her eyes turned toward the heavy closed drapes over the window. "Indeed, I have almost forgotten what a sunny day looks like."

Once my eyes adjusted to the darkness, I was able to take in her entirely black gown with full-length gloves and black scarf wound around her head, making it easy to believe her statement. I was tempted to ask then and there what drove her into hiding so thoroughly but sensed that the time was not right.

"You are a student at King's College?" she asked, refocusing on me with effort.

"Yes, ma'am, studying law," I answered.

"As was I before..." she said, again looking toward the window. She recovered more quickly this time, though, and continued. "This is a high-paying position because I am paying for your discretion as much as for your work reading to my father."

I glanced toward the large doors that must lead to her father's master bedroom.

She followed my glance, brow furrowed. "My father is very ill and requires my constant care. But I need relief as well, and that is where you come in." She pulled out a sheet of paper. "These rules must be adhered to, to the letter. Once you have read them all, please initial next to each line, and sign at the bottom."

I took the paper from her. "This will be the contract between us," she added, "and should you in any way, at any time, diverge from these rules, your employment with me will be immediately terminated."

I nodded. "May I take this home and examine it first, Miss Barclay?"

"I expect no less," she agreed, rising. "Will you let me know by tomorrow,?"

"I will," I said, extending my hand.

She looked blankly down at my hand for a moment, as I guessed she would, then smiled wanly and bowed. I withdrew my hand thoughtfully and did the same, then left with a head full of questions.

*   *   *

The next day I copied word-for-word Miss Barclay's list of rules into my new notebook on the case. I had initialed beside each line as I went, fully intending to agree to her demands *in toto*.

I signed the document and then folded it up, replacing it in my purse.

Only then did I allow myself full study of her demands:
1. Never turn on any lights or open the drapes. A candle will always be provided, and should it go out, matches sit beside it.
2. The reading chair should never be moved.
3. Please restrict your own movements to the reading chair. Do not walk around the rooms.
4. Do not touch my father or interact with him in any way other than reading to him.
5. Do not touch me.
6. Do not speak of me or my father to anyone outside this household.
7. Do not touch any of the articles in this room.
8. Do not bring anything into the room with you, save a book, which can be of your own choosing.

I read over these very strange, very exacting instructions a few times. The main requirements seemed to revolve around proximity — to herself and to her father. Walking over to my bookcase, I picked through some of my grandfather's medical journals, seeking the one that spoke of psychological illnesses.

Perhaps her phobias could be diagnosed. But after looking through several case studies, though I found some supporting documentation of a fear of darkness, I could find nothing to explain a fear of touching, only a paragraph about the fear of crowds, so I closed the book with a sigh. I would have to consult in person with a doctor to pursue the theory.

I decided to head out on my morning walk, mulling over the problem as I made my way toward the Barclays' home. Did Miss Barclay fear for her father's safety or my own? I did not think Mr. Barclay would risk my exposure to an illness if he thought his father was contagious, but what did I really know about the man? It seemed passing strange to allow me into the room alone, but worry about my distance from the patient. Was there something I was not to see up close? Some sign of abuse? Perhaps his weakness made him more susceptible to illness I might be carrying? Miss Barclay might have refused to shake hands with me for the same reason — worry that I might unknowingly infect her and then she pass on that disease to her father.

By now I had arrived at the house and was greeted by the same taciturn butler, who silently took my signed papers.

"Sir, not to intrude, but your foot," I spoke up, surprising him, "don't you think it is time to have it looked at?"

"I *beg* your pardon?" he replied, not even glancing down at where I pointed, his tone icy to the point of Antarctic temperatures.

"Untreated, gout can lead to even more serious health issues," I said, pursing my lips at the ugly look that appeared very briefly on the man's face at the word 'gout'.

Obviously, he did not like that I had noticed his limp, but he said nothing and simply nodded with glittering, angry eyes. I had made it back down the front stairs and onto the sidewalk when he called out to me by name.

"Miss Barclay wonders if you could perchance start your service right now," he said in a sonorous voice, his face expressionless once more.

I agreed with surprise and re-entered the house, following him up the stairs as he purposely put full weight on his right foot despite the pain it must have caused him. But instead of taking me to the rooms I had visited the day before, he directed me to the library, explaining that Miss Barclay expected me to pick out a book to read to his master. I went in and was only slightly surprised to see Mr. Barclay sitting comfortably in the room.

He, however, did not seem taken aback at all, and rose to say, "Ah, you must be my father's new caregiver ... miss?"

"Adams," I said, playing along.

"Ah, Miss Adams," he said, with a nod to the butler who stood waiting in the doorway.

"I am looking for a suitable book to read your father today," I explained.

He smiled, reaching for the book he had just now been reading. "This is one of my favorites, please read this one to him. The whole story, if you please, he does so enjoy it."

And so saying, with a bow he handed me a thick, hardbound cover.

I took it, once again charmed by his manners, and followed the butler out of the library and all the way to the room where I had met Miss Barclay the day before. Again, she sat in the shadows, and again she was swathed head to toe in black.

"Miss Barclay," I said in greeting, taking note of her pale skin and tired eyes and comparing this to her brother's vibrant eyes and strong jaw. I suspected her to be within five years of my own age, but worry had added dark circles under her eyes and tensed her mouth beyond her years.

"Ah, Portia, then you are clear on our agreement?" she asked, brandishing the signed paper I had just dropped off.

I noticed her fingernails before I answered: very pale, with only the slightest hint of pink, though it was hard to tell for sure in the limited candlelight.

"I am clear, and eager to help," I answered honestly.

She nodded, lips pursed thoughtfully, as she silently considered me.

"Very well. You have a book, splendid, let us go in." She stood, slightly unsteady. I reached out to steady her and then remembered rule number five and withdrew my aid. She watched my entire action with narrowed eyes, and only when my hand was back at my side did she move again.

With her candle in hand, she led me to the door, past an oak wardrobe and a matching screen and desk that, I was startled to notice, had chains and a lock around the elegant brass handles. They had been all but invisible in the darkness of the antechamber, and I watched as she fished a key from a necklace around her neck. She applied the key to the door's lock with care, her hands trembling slightly.

Inside were, thankfully, more candles than were in the outer room, though in such a large bedroom their light was hard-pressed to change the somber mood. The drapes were, like their peers just outside, firmly closed against the daylight, and only by squinting could I make out the features of the figure in the bed.

He shared his daughter's sickly pallor, though much more so, and his features seemed stretched over the bones of his narrow face. His eyes were open, but he didn't seem to see us, mumbling instead to himself in a low undertone.

She took a few steps into the room and then pointed me to the high-backed chair near the door, beside which sat a large, fat candle.

"Father, we have a visitor. This is Miss Portia Adams, and she has kindly come to read to you today," she said as she continued past me to the bed.

If he heard her words, there was no indication, so I dutifully took my seat as Miss Barclay moved closer to her father. She whispered into his ear, and the mumbling stopped for a moment. She took a rag from the side table and carefully swabbed at his face, whispering the whole time. I pretended to be paying attention to the book in my hands, but regarding them both from under my lashes, I took note of their interaction.

Miss Barclay's actions did not seem to me to be odd; in fact, this was the most normal her behavior had been. She was bent over her father, still talking to him, and I could see that he was not flinching away from her touch. His eyes flickered as she spoke, so it seemed he comprehended her words, though he could not answer.

She had just moved to cleaning around her father's lips when she suddenly jerked away with a gasp.

"You must leave ... immediately!" she whispered to me, backing away from the bed, where the poor man resumed his murmuring soliloquy.

"Now?" I replied, wondering what had happened, trying to see around her body to his face. "But—"

"No time to explain," she said, pulling me forcefully by the arm, forgetting her own rule and rushing us back out the door. She closed it and tried unsuccessfully to apply the key to the lock twice, but her hands were shaking too badly.

On her third attempt I finally said, "Miss Barclay, if you will hand me your key for a moment, I will lock the door for you."

She glanced up at me and I was surprised to recognize fear in her tired eyes, before she grudgingly handed me the key. Noting the blood on the rag she had been using on her father's face, I quickly locked the door and handed the key back to her directly. She had regained a bit of her composure and tucked the rag out of sight as she backed away from the locked door.

"Apologies, this must seem very strange to you," she said, moving slowly back toward the chairs.

To deny it would have been both disingenuous and suspicious, so I admitted it. "It does. You seem suddenly more worried about your father, more so than when we entered the room. Shall we call a doctor?"

"No!" she exclaimed, and then regaining her composure, shut her eyes wearily. "I cannot explain. Please do not ask me to explain, for I cannot."

I did not want to push her on this our second meeting so I said instead, "Very well then, I will not intrude on your business."

I stood, bowed slightly to her and headed for the door, leaving her to the darkness and her own dark worries.

CHAPTER THREE

Constable Dawes and I often consulted each other on the crimes and cases that interested us. His pursuits were entirely professional and sanctioned, being a junior member of Scotland Yard. Mine were known by few and supported by even fewer. That said, I flattered myself that someday this interest and experience would be useful in my professional life.

Once a week, I was invited to dinner with my downstairs tenants, and on one such night, Brian and I were swapping stories from our week's travails.

"But surely she is guilty. She was caught with the murder weapon — fleeing the scene!" he said over the table.

"I understand, but how did she manage to so violently kill the victim?" I challenged him as Mrs. Dawes laid the table around us, turning up the radio as she passed behind her husband, who was nodding off again. "You said that she was barely one hundred pounds! The victim was almost twice her size and was struck from behind by a single blow to his neck. Is she six feet tall, with extraordinary upper body strength?"

"No," he admitted. "She's tiny, smaller than you for certain, closer to five feet than six."

"Then how did she get up high enough to stab him with the amount of force required to kill a man with one blow?" I raised my hand high above me head in a stabbing motion. I demonstrated stabbing upwards with my butter knife and then gripped the knife and stabbed downwards.

"Perhaps he was bending down at the time?" Brian offered, scratching his chin, a smile coming to his lips at my pantomime.

"I would need to see the crime scene, but the position of the body as it falls from a kneeling position as compared to when a man is standing is quite marked," I replied. "I refer you to casebook #122 upstairs for details on how the body falls after being struck and common bruising when it hits the ground."

He considered, then nodded. "I will borrow that casebook from you after supper, thank you, most helpful. Now tell me about this strange case you say you are bound by secrecy not to tell me about. You know I can be relied upon to keep a secret."

I nodded, knowing that his career made him one of the few people I could share this case with.

"I have been asked to discover the real reason behind a young woman's complete withdrawal from society. She is under severe stress due to the illness of a loved one, but it is suspected that there is more to her change in personality than stress, though from my first day on the job, I will admit that the illness caused me not a little stress myself," I said, thinking back.

That strange day at the Barclays', closing the door behind me, I had walked back down the stairs, collected my things from the butler and left the house.

About a block away, Mr. Barclay came into sight and fell into step beside me, the rain starting almost in parallel with his appearance at my side.

"I hope you have some explanation for placing me in such danger, sir," I said angrily, not slowing my pace but pulling my hat lower over my eyes to deflect the droplets.

He looked shocked at my statement and paled slightly. "Why, whatever can you mean, Miss Adams? You were never in any danger!"

"Blood on the lips, weight loss, general weakness," I listed, still walking briskly. "You may not know this, but when my mother became ill and went undiagnosed for months, I did extensive research in search of the cause of her illness. Your father shows some of the tell-tale symptoms of tuberculosis, and it is something you should have divulged."

Oddly, my explanation seemed to relieve him, because his paleness receded as he shook his head vehemently, little drops of water flying off his hat as he did so. "Oh no, Miss Adams, I assure you, tuberculosis was the first thing the doctors tested for, months and months ago — along with cholera, malaria, the Black Death, influenza, the grippe ... the list of diseases systematically eliminated was the length of my arm!"

I finally slowed so that I could look the man in the eye; he seemed sincere.

"Well," I hesitated before saying, "I would never claim to be a medical expert, and if I have wrongfully accused you of endangering my life, I will, of course, apologize."

He had raised his hands. "No, no apology necessary, I want to wipe every doubt from your mind so as to allow you to concentrate on my sister."

I recalled blushing at this reminder of what I was actually being paid to investigate, and when he extended his arm, I humbly took it.

"Do you know of Dr. Joyce? He is a family friend, and his offices are a quick cab ride away. Let him tell you with his own lips of his findings," he offered, and he hailed a cab as he spoke. It was still midday and the traffic was minimal, so we were quickly picked up and transported to the grand offices of the aforementioned Dr. Joyce. The building, according its cornerstone, was almost a hundred years old, but the marble pillars and cornices that led up the stairs to the ornate iron doors were newer and very expensive.

Shaking hands with the middle-aged gentleman, I was introduced as a schoolfellow who had taken up a part-time position in the Barclay household.

"Ah," said the doctor, as he offered us upholstered chairs in front of his ornate desk, "very good! Then your sister has somewhat relaxed her policies, Barclay?"

"Only very slightly, sir," Barclay answered. "And actually it is more for Miss Adams' benefit that we are here. She expressed concern about possible contagion through employment in our home."

"Oh, very understandable, Miss Adams, and one can never be too careful with one's health," the doctor said approvingly. "But as far as I or any of my colleagues can tell..." He leaned over his papers to turn on his desk lamp since the cloudy day afforded little light in this office, despite the large windows. The doctor drew out a folder, consulted it under the light then continued. "The Right Honorable Judge Barclay remains undiagnosed but not contagious. None of us who have been around him, examined him and spoken to him have developed any symptoms, including the members of the family and the staff who serve them."

"As I said, the list of diseases he is not suffering from is long and covers tuberculosis, cholera and influenza," Barclay offered as explanation.

"And many, many others," the doctor said, taking up the thread. "If I could show you the chart in my hands without breaking confidentiality with my patient, I would. But you will have to take my word for it that whatever Judge Barclay is suffering from, poor man, it is not contractible by touch or breath."

"As I admitted to Mr. Barclay moments ago, I am, of course, not a medical expert," I replied. "But Elaine Barclay seems to be developing a few of the same symptoms as her father, does she not?"

"Not unless something has changed in the past few weeks with the poor girl," answered the doctor, and he then looked to Mr. Barclay for confirmation.

"Miss Adams is no doubt speaking of the tired look my sister has about her and the paleness of her features." He paused, and I remember nodding — that was indeed what I had been referring to. "Those are the symptoms that you tried to talk to her about in June, sir," Barclay finished with a sigh.

"Ah yes," the doctor confirmed. "Miss Elaine Barclay is indeed suffering a malaise, but I suspect it to be mental as opposed to physical. When we considered that Judge Barclay might in fact be contagious, I had blood drawn and full work-ups of the entire family conducted back in..." he consulted his chart again, "...February of this year. Nothing was found. I believe that Miss Barclay's choice to shutter herself in her house and dwell in misery is due to some mental issues, and that is what is causing the outward symptoms you have described."

"What about the possibility that I could be bringing germs into contact with a weakened man ... and Miss Barclay's strong aversion to sunlight?"

The doctor thoughtfully leaned back in his chair. "I would not disagree that the patient may have a weakened immune system that requires us to be extra careful around him. But as to the banishment of light — that as far as I can tell is not a symptom but a situation that Miss Barclay has imposed on herself and her father, initiated without medical basis or advice."

Barclay looked at his hands at that, and then said, "There were the burns a few months ago, doctor..."

"Oh, come now, very minor skin irritation, the effects of which were gone the next day," the doctor answered, shaking his head and then, answering my puzzled look, he went on to say, "Back at the beginning of his illness, Miss Adams, Judge Barclay suffered some unexplained burns on the backs of his hands while on his way, I believe, to an appointment with me."

"And Miss Barclay has taken that small occurrence and made it into a symptom so worrying that she has condemned them both to darkness?" I asked.

"It certainly seems that way," the doctor answered. "And I promise you, we did our best to talk her out of it. Doctor Alan Roche, if you will recall, Mr. Barclay, attended your home every morning for two weeks in the hopes of convincing Miss Barclay that she was doing more harm than good. But all it resulted in was his being barred from the house!"

I thought back to the way Miss Barclay had locked the doors behind us, and tilted my head. "Thank you, Dr. Joyce, this has been most enlightening."

"Not at all, young lady, and if you wish to speak to any of the other four physicians involved in the case, I would be happy to arrange for it."

He then turned to Barclay as he linked his hands and leaned back toward us. "Does this mean I will be permitted to examine my patient again?"

I recalled how Mr. Barclay looked saddened. "I wish that were true, Dr. Joyce, but my sister still refuses to move on this decision."

"There may come a time, young man, when you may need to countermand your sister's orders ... for the very life of your father!" the doctor answered angrily, slamming his folder shut.

"So the illness is not contagious," Brian now said, dragging my attention back to the present.

"No, at least it is not any known disease," I replied.

Brian chewed on that, along with his dinner, for a moment. "So, which is it? Is she protecting this man from you and if so, why let you in the room at all?"

"That's just it, Brian, I don't think she was protecting him — I think she was protecting us."

CHAPTER FOUR

All this talk of protecting me or not protecting me, combined with Brian's off-hand remark about being a 'capable woman', reminded me of the promise I had made to my guardian concerning my education in self-defense.

So when one of my afternoon classes was cancelled during the week, I found myself wandering in Brixton, where I knew the former boxer lived.

Despite being a transplanted Canadian, the fact that I looked like a Londoner until I opened my mouth and revealed my 'colonial accent' meant that I had been able to walk the streets of this populated city with relative invisibility. Not so in Brixton. I was obviously and immediately the minority, getting looks from the local black population and feeling quite out of place as soon as I exited the tube stop.

A couple around my age passed me, their eyes suspicious, whispering to each other as soon as they were out of my sight, and a group of small boys wearing brightly colored scarves started from their game of jacks as I passed their sport, pointing at me and calling to each other to see the odd sight of a white woman walking alone in Brixton.

Digging into the bottom of my ever-present satchel, I again consulted the small piece of paper upon which Mrs. Jones had written the man's address, and with a deep breath I knocked on the painted wooden door to the brick house. The house was large, with three stories that looked as though they had been built by very different builders with varying amounts of money and architectural styles.

"Eh, what's up?" said a voice from somewhere to my left.

Poking his bald head out of a downstairs apartment, I recognized Asher Jenkins. "Up here, Mr. Jenkins. Portia Adams, remember?"

He flashed a huge grin when he recognized me, waggling a thick finger as he came up the wooden stairs to meet me at street-level. "I said you were pert — and I was right, wasn't I? Comin' all the way down here on yer own. Does anyone even know you were comin'?"

I shook my head, annoyed now and somewhat regretting this promise. "No, but surely you aren't saying that your neighbors are a threat to me, are you, Mr. Jenkins?"

He guffawed, shaking his head and waving me down the stairs into his basement flat, where the smells of sweat and blood combined and assaulted the senses.

I looked down at the padded mats at my feet that were scattered all around this front room and wondering what I had gotten myself into. I could see that there were two other rooms leading out of this large room, which I expected were the bedroom and bathroom, respectively.

"Does my guardian come here often?" I asked, removing my jacket and putting it on the hook by the door where he had pointed. "Mrs. Jones is the one who asked you to give me these lessons, after all. Do you two socialize much?"

He shrugged his big shoulders as I removed my hat. "Less so now than when we were young, t'be sure. She is a traveler, your Mrs. Jones is — she hasn't lived in London for a long time — and I've hardly lived anywhere else."

"So then, did you know her husbands?" I asked, following as he walked around the large room, noticing the multitude of rectangular windows ringing the open space, allowing in the maximum amount of light for a sublevel apartment.

"Her husbands?" he repeated, the wrinkles around his eyes deepening as he stopped, picking up a wooden chair and moving it against a wall. "Which husband is it you're talkin' about?"

"Really, any of them," I hedged, running my hand along the wooden bar that had been screwed into the wall, reminding me a crude dancer's bar in a ballet studio. "I know she married someone in London, and divorced him, and then married someone else in San Francisco, where she and my grandmother were friends."

"Mmm-hmm, and you've asked her about this, have you?" He raised his chin in a challenge.

I sighed. "Mr. Jenkins, if you don't want to answer my questions..."

"I do not," he answered immediately. "That is not what we are here for. My first lesson, little lady, is this: your first line of defense is to never let yourself be caught in a dangerous situation. So that starts with gettin' smart about lookin' around you, payin' attention to the people, the exits, the weapons at hand.

"Your second option is to carry a gun. Is that possible?" he asked, cracking his knuckles.

"I don't think I am anywhere near that worried about my personal safety," I said. "I am still hopeful to replace the gun option with the running away option. I have no illusions of bravery or prowess in the physical arena."

He laughed. "You have decent skills in 'that area', as you put it, little one, with those blue eyes, and dark hair — your grandmother used that kind of physical prowess to get herself, and me on more than one occasion, out of very sticky situations."

I blushed at his compliment and thought of my mother and her kind blue eyes and felt a slight pang that the color was not as clear in my memory as it once had been.

"So, no gun means that we'll focus on the element of surprise, so as to fell your adversary quickly rather than engaging in a drawn-out physical battle you are unlikely to win," he said.

Far from being hurt by his most logical assessment, I heartily agreed, and then asked, "Was it your father or your brother who coaxed you into boxing?"

"My father," he answered automatically. "How did you know it was in the family?"

I pointed to the large bag hanging from the ceiling. "That bag is a more than a decade old at least, and so is the chain holding it. And the height of that bag — it gets lowered and raised to two specific heights consistently, one for you at about six foot two, and another for someone closer to my height — I'd guess under five foot ten."

Mr. Jenkins ran his fingers over the well-worn chain holding the punching bag, "My father was small for a boxer, but that man!" He laughed again, a deep, warm sound. "That man could surprise the devil himself with his left hook!"

He glanced at me. "You're a righty, eh, Adams?" I nodded. "That's what everyone expects, you know, and we'll work on that, but we're also gonna learn ya one mean left hook. No one'll expect that from ya!"

And Mr. Jenkins was as good as his word, launching right into the basics of anticipating and dodging attacks. We practiced footwork, what to do if someone grabs you from behind, and most of all, how to deal with a heavyweight restraining you.

"That's their biggest advantage," he growled as I swung away from his grappling hands. "Once they get their weight on top of ye, fight's about ten times harder to win."

"So?" I gasped, ducking again breathlessly. "What do I do?"

"Stay outta their reach, just like you're doin' now," he growled back, pivoting and coming at me from the left this time and trapping me against the wall. "Always remember, you're a woman, they're expecting an easy mark, so don't make it easy, and most blokes'll just give up. And if God forbid they get you between a rock n' a hard place, I got a few more tricks for ya."

CHAPTER FIVE

That weekend I decided this case required more data. Quick research had given me enough information on Elaine's ex-fiancé, Mr. Ridley, to know that on Saturdays he did shift work at a hospice in central London.

Borrowing from one of the many disguises in the attic, I found a suitable nurse's uniform (though which of the previous tenants of this apartment could have fit into this costume, I knew not) and used makeup to age my features, even applying some white paint at my temples.

I was at this stage of my *maquillage* when my guardian knocked at the door and entered.

She stopped at seeing me thus, bent in front of the mirror, and then I saw a slow grin spread across her face.

"What are you up to now?" she asked, pulling off her coat and coming to stand beside me in front of the mirror, her various rings glinting, marking a recent cleaning.

"I have a case," I explained, looking at myself critically in the mirror. "What do you think, do I look like a middle-aged nurse?"

She snorted and, grasping my chin, pulled a few loose tendrils from my tight bun and rubbed some purplish makeup lightly under my eyes. She adjusted my makeup with a small brush and had me try on a few different pairs of shoes before she was done.

"Walk like your feet ache from years of walking up and down hospital halls and be sure to be very deferential to all the doctors," she advised as she worked.

"What was this costume used for before, do you know?" I asked, looking up as she directed.

"I'm sure I have no idea," she said airily. "But I am certainly enjoying imagining John dressed as a nurse instead of a doctor for once!

"I hear you had a highly successful first bout with Jenkins," she prompted, tapping out some makeup on her hand and applying it to my face.

"'Bout' is the right word for it," I admitted. "I have more than a few bruises from the encounter."

"But it was useful, *non*?" she asked, turning my face so our eyes met again. "You will be going back?"

"Every Tuesday afternoon, ma'am, I promise," I answered. "And I have to admit, much of what Mr. Jenkins said about paying attention to your surroundings and keeping exits in view was quite fascinating. He has an interesting paranoia about everyday life."

She snorted. "Justified, I promise you." She stepped back to admire her work. "Now, what is this case?"

I hesitated, as I had when speaking to Brian. I had, after all, given my word to Mr. Barclay and then separately to Miss Barclay.

"Oh, come now, you've been sighted about town on the arm of the very handsome, very eligible James Barclay. Surely this case has something to do with his father's mysterious illness?" she prodded, leading me back to the fireplace.

I sighed. Sometimes having highly intelligent, highly connected people in your life was trying. I brightened when I considered that she probably thought the same thing.

"Actually, I am not hired to investigate anything about poor Judge Barclay. His case is one for the doctors, I am afraid," I said, pulling on a threadbare overcoat.

"No, I've been asked to try to discern if there is something more than concern behind Miss Barclay's drastic personality change."

"Elaine Barclay?" My guardian asked, her perfect silver eyebrows arched. "How very interesting. I had heard that she broke off her engagement to Mr. Ridley, but assumed it was a result of family disapproval."

I had by now put on a hat to complete the ensemble. "Why? Is there aught about Mr. Ridley I should know?"

"Oh, dear no, he is a most agreeable gentleman," she answered, settling herself comfortably by the fireplace with a sigh. "Both gentleman are, though Ridley is a much more suitable match for you than Barclay, if you ask me, despite the latter being the richer of the two."

I rolled my eyes.

"All right, I will pretend that these two eligible men are not so eligible," she said with a chuckle. "I am referring to the well-known fact that Elaine and James do not get on. Even more so after she got engaged, from what I was hearing at the season's parties."

I compared this to Barclay's description of his sister. "Odd ... that is not the impression I got from speaking to James Barclay."

"That is very interesting then, little one," she said, pulling an ottoman close. "Now, you do your investigating. I'm going to take a nap so that when you return I'm full of energy to hear about your adventure!"

*   *   *

When I arrived back at 221 Baker Street, it was almost suppertime. I trudged up the stairs and was pleasantly surprised to find a warm meal on the stove and my guardian still waiting for me.

I apologized for my tardiness between gulps of delicious onion soup and fresh bread, and only when I had consumed my fill did I lean back from the table with a satisfied exhalation.

"That," I declared, "was exactly what I needed."

"I thought as much," she said with a smile, pulling out her tiny ceramic pipe and lighting it. "How did your day pretending to be a nurse go?"

I wearily rose and stepped behind the screen to undress. "Difficult. And I remain firmly in my chosen career — the medical gene seems to have been lost to me, no matter who my grandfather was."

"Never mind, dear, there are at least two other Watsons carrying on that family tradition," she said from the other side of the screen. "Did John Watson come by and visit again by the way?"

"Yes, I thought I told you! And his brother invited me to dinner next week."

"Lovely boys," my guardian said. "You should go. They are men worthy of being part of your life, those two are. And maybe they could even help you with your current case. How did it go with Dr. Ridley?"

In a much more comfortable long skirt, blouse and cardigan, I rejoined her, scrubbing at my face with a wet towel. "Not well, I'm sad to say. My questions about his ex-fiancée were met with anger. All he would say was that his opinion of women had been forever changed by the experience."

"Oh my," my guardian said. "That sounds like their parting was acrimonious and not perhaps caused by the brother's disapproval at all?"

I shook my head. "That was my impression, at least — that Mr. Ridley blames Elaine Barclay directly for the dissolution of their engagement."

"Interesting," was all she said.

"I did manage, over the course of a very long shift, to turn the conversation toward Judge Barclay," I said, sitting forward, "but Ridley claims to have had limited access to his, well, his future father-in-law at the time, I suppose. He said that his questions to Elaine Barclay were met with increasing suspicion and paranoia."

"I wonder if his poking and prodding around her father's illness could have led Elaine to break things off," Mrs. Jones mused.

"I wondered the same thing, though there was no diplomatic way to ask that, of course," I said. "But surely a worried daughter would seek out and encourage more medical intervention, not less — especially from someone she trusted enough to consider marrying?"

"Then where does that leave you?" she asked, taking a puff of her little pipe.

"Right back to my stolen moments in that gloomy room," I answered with a sigh. "I think the answers to this case are hiding in there like shadows in a dark alley."

"Speaking of dark alleys," she started and then poked me in the arm when I rolled my eyes, knowing where she was going with this, "we were supposed to continue our tour of downtown London, were we not?"

"I have been just a little busy, Mrs. Jones," I replied.

"With school work?" she demanded. "Or with this new case?"

"Both," I retorted tartly, and then, "and also with my efforts to track down Sherlock Holmes."
That took her aback and she actually started in her chair.

"That surprises you, Mrs. Jones?" I asked, though I had meant to test her. "I am, as you know, on a quest to find out more about my grandparents. Mr. Holmes knew my grandfather better than anyone alive, other than his own sons, with whom, as I said, I am sitting down with again next week. The great detective is the next logical next step, don't you think?"

"I ... hadn't considered it," she replied, tapping her pipe on the ashtray, her trembling hand evident in the way the ashes missed their target.

She cursed aloud, another telling sign of her discomfort, and I rose to get my brush and dustpan, calling over my shoulder, "You don't by chance know where Mr. Holmes is, do you, Mrs. Jones? So far Brian's efforts to locate him have failed, even with the members of the constabulary who knew the man."

I had by now returned to her side and swept up the errant ashes, waiting for her reply.

"No, I do not," she answered when I looked at her.

I nodded, having surmised as much, though the reason for her obviously defensive feelings on the matter still evaded me.

"It's interesting," I said, returning to my kitchenette and tilting the dustpan over my dustbin as I spoke, "you only ever speak of half of the detective team who lived here. I've hardly heard you mention Holmes at all."

"Well, I focus on answering questions about your grandfather, of course," she replied hurriedly.

"Obviously," I answered, returning to sit back at her side, "but now you must tell me what you know of Sherlock Holmes. Please."

She surprised me by leaning forward to say, "Agreed — but let's start with your efforts as aided by the young constable from downstairs — what have you two found out and who have you talked to?"

CHAPTER SIX

The next day I returned to the Barclay residence and was once again shown to the library by the surly butler. This time Mr. Barclay was not there, so I purposely picked a different book off the shelf, one I knew well, and followed the butler to the master bedroom.

After I knocked on the door, the butler, looking even paler than usual, motioned me in to find Miss Barclay once more sitting in candlelit darkness and dressed all in black.

"Ah, Portia!" she said, her tired face reflecting surprise. "I confess I was worried that after that ... incident the other day that you would not return."

"Not at all, Miss Barclay, confused as I remain about what happened, you hired me to do a job, and I am here to do it."

"Very well, shall we proceed then?" I nodded and watched as she again produced the key from the chain around her neck. As before, when we entered the room it was dark and candlelit. I obediently sat straight down in the chair I knew to be assigned to me and started to read aloud. I had been reading for perhaps fifteen minutes when there came a knock on the outer door.

Elaine looked at me, hesitated, and then glanced at her father where he lay prone on the bed.

The knock came again, and she made up her mind. Passing me, she headed back through the previously locked door into the anteroom where she spent her days and answered the outer door.

I continued to read aloud, but from my vantage point I could see the maid enter the room carrying a tray. Elaine waited impatiently for the maid to put down the tray, and then she took a look at me to make sure I was still in the same position. I was, of course, and I continued to read as she watched me from the other room.

She finally stepped out of my sight, and only the slight aroma of food seeping into the air alerted me to the fact that the tray held the midday meal.

I continued to read, squinting at the bed as I did so, careful not to move or give Elaine reason to worry. When I stopped hearing utensils being used, I carefully leaned back in my chair and could see her out of the corner of my eye, weeping over her half-finished meal.

I had picked this book purposefully, knowing the words well enough that I barely needed to glance at the page to continue my recitation. This allowed me to observe her movements in the anteroom while she had the comfort of hearing my voice doing the job I had been hired to do. I glanced at Judge Barclay and could see that the man was either unconscious or asleep.

I leaned forward again as she stood and walked out of my sight toward where I knew the tall wardrobe stood on the north side of the room. Assuming she was searching for a kerchief to stem her tears, I was surprised to see, as she walked back toward us, something small in her hands, something that reflected light ... a glass? No, too small to be a glass. It looked like a ... salt shaker without a metal cover ... some kind of small glass container ... it was hard to tell from across two rooms with so little light.

She leaned over the tray with her back to me for a few seconds. When she turned, tray in hand, the glass container was nowhere to be seen.

I kept reading as she passed me and carefully placed the tray on the side table near the bed.

"That is all for today I think, Portia," she said, her back to me. "Thank you, please come again tomorrow."

I dutifully stopped, placing the bookmark to hold my place and leaving the book on the table beside my designated chair.

She was leaning over her father, so I carefully stepped into the anteroom. Noting the half-finished plate, and not seeing the glass object, I stepped to the wardrobe to test its door. It was locked, and I dared not linger and incite Miss Barclay's suspicion, so I went out the door into the relief of the sunny hallway.

I made my way out of the house and back onto the street, considering my data. What was that glass object? Was it relevant to this case? Could it be that Elaine Barclay was on some kind of drug? Opium addiction? I made a mental note to look into my grandfather's medical books for symptoms of drug addiction. I shook my head and the afternoon scene swam dizzily before my eyes. I stopped walking, leaning on a lamppost, suddenly sure I was going to be sick.

"Why, Miss Adams!" said a voice in front of me.

I opened my eyes, still battling the dizzy spell, and saw James Barclay striding toward me looking very concerned.

I had the chance to observe some papers sticking out of his suit pocket before I knew no more.

*   *   *

I awoke in my own bed to find Mrs. Dawes slumbering in the chair beside me. I glanced at my window, surprised to see how dark it was, and sitting up carefully, I reached for a water glass beside me, waking Mrs. Dawes from her nap with a start.

"Well, finally, missy," she said, leaning forward to test my forehead. "No fever still — how are you feeling?"

"Tired, but well, Mrs. Dawes. How did I get here? And where are my clothes?" I asked, looking down at the simple cotton dress I now wore.

"That fine gentleman Mr. Barclay brought you in, didn't he? Carried you all the way up the stairs," she said, adjusting my blanket. "Most worried he was 'bout you, little lady, most worried. Even insisted that I bathe your arms and legs in case you were catching fever."

"How long ago was that?" I asked, putting down my glass and doing a bit of a self-assessment, detecting none of the dizziness I had felt before.

"Three hours you've been asleep," Mrs. Dawes replied, nodding at my surprised look. "Your Mrs. Jones was here when he brought you in and stayed with Mr. Barclay and me the first little while. But when you wouldn't wake up, she ran out to find a doctor. She asked me to stay here with you in case you woke up, and thank goodness you have!"

"Oh, Portia!" declared Mrs. Jones as she entered the flat with her usual dramatic flourish. "You're awake finally! What happened?"

"I don't know, to be honest," I replied, allowing her to check me over, noticing the familiar-looking gentleman who had followed her up the stairs and now stood just at my doorway. "I left the Barclays, got dizzy, and I suppose ... fainted?"

"Fainted? That's what poor Mr. Barclay said, but I just can't believe it," she repeated incredulously. "Portia Constance Adams, you are *not* the fainting type. I don't believe it."

Mrs. Dawes took the opportunity to steal out of the room, promising to bring up a spot of tea, and taking the gentleman's top hat and coat as she passed, revealing his medical bag as she did so.

"I am fine, ma'am, really," I said, reaching over to pat her hand. "And Dr. Watson, please do come in," I called to the man at the door, my uncle.

"Miss Adams," replied Hamish Watson, brother to the Watson I had already met, "I am sorry our first meeting is under these circumstances."

Mrs. Jones waved him into the room, so he approached to take my extended hand in greeting. While he was looking over my vitals, opening my eyes wide, and taking my pulse, I ran my eyes over him, comparing his physical attributes to the photos I had seen of our shared grandfather. Where I looked almost nothing like John Watson, this fellow looked like a rounder version of the man.

Dr. Hamish Watson was in his forties, younger than my mother, which made sense since she was the product of John Watson's first marriage and this man a product of Watson's third. He had a very round face, a receding dark brown hairline and brown eyes that wrinkled when he concentrated, as he was now, looking at his watch with his hand on my wrist. He was shorter than I and had the look of someone suited to desk work rather than physical activity, leading me to believe that he hadn't followed his father's example of joining the military.

"It's this case, isn't it?" Mrs. Jones pressed as Dr. Watson pulled a stethoscope out of his bag and with my permission applied it to my chest. "It's the stress of school and cases and God knows what else! You frightened Mr. Barclay silly. You should have seen him when he carried you in here — white as a sheet!"

"I am sorry to have scared anyone," I said, and meant it, taking a breath as the doctor instructed. "I am at a loss as to what caused it. As far as I can tell, I have no other symptoms."

Mrs. Jones looked to the doctor for his assessment, and he cleared his throat. "Miss Adams is correct, I see no underlying health issues. Her lungs sound clear, her pulse is steady, her pupils are slightly dilated but not worryingly so. How are you feeling right now, miss?"

I took another breath, sitting up fully and swinging my legs over the side of my bed. "Fine, honestly, I feel totally fine."

"Did you ingest anything odd recently or something you had not eaten or drunk before?" he prompted.

"Nothing out of the ordinary here at home, and I neither ate nor drank at the Barclays'," I replied, shaking my head. From the stairs came the sound of loud footsteps and a few seconds later, an out-of-breath Brian Dawes came into the room, his hair disheveled and his boots leaving wet track marks on the carpeting at my bedroom door.

"I ... I was at the pub after work ... I just got home ... my mother just told me..." he blurted out in a rush, glancing between Mrs. Jones and Dr. Watson, his gaze finally landing on me.

"I'm fine, Mr. Dawes, really," I said, raising my hand toward him palm out, hoping to impart some calm, but at the same time embarrassed that he had heard about my fainting spell.

"Oh ... all right, good," he replied, recovering his breath. "Apologies, Mrs. Jones, sir."

Mrs. Jones managed a small smile. "Not at all, Mr. Dawes, you were just worried about my charge, and for that I am appreciative. The doctor was just delivering his diagnosis though, so..." She looked to the other gentleman in the room.

Dr. Watson shrugged, replacing his stethoscope in his bag. "Then I think your guardian is right, Miss Adams, we should just chalk this up to the stress of a new country, new school and new surroundings."

"And needless cases," Mrs. Jones put in, causing the doctor to cock his eyebrow at her disapproving tone.

"Thank you, so much, Dr. Watson, for coming down here to check on me," I said, extending both hands his way, "and I very much look forward to meeting the rest of your family next week." He bowed at the waist, smiled at both of us and turned on his heel, medical bag in hand.

"Doesn't matter anyways, does it, miss?" Mrs. Dawes said, negotiating her way around her son, who still stood dripping in my bedroom doorway, to deliver the promised pot of tea. "I suppose Mr. Barclay's advice of getting you cleaned up and cool worked!"

I recovered quickly from whatever had ailed me, and the next day Mr. Barclay visited.

"Miss Adams!" he exclaimed when I answered the door. "I am very pleased to see you up and about!"

"Yes, thanks to you, sir," I replied, ushering him in and noticing he wasn't wearing cologne today. Taking a closer look at his appearance, I also noticed his tie had been knotted in a hurry, the lengths slightly wrong and the knot too loose. Had my fainting spell scared him that badly? "I am most grateful for your help yesterday. If you had not come along when you did..."

He shook his head modestly. "Not at all, Miss Adams. Had I but known that you were coming by the house, I would have stayed home instead of visiting an ill friend."

I filed that away, remembering the pieces of paper I had seen sticking out of his jacket before I fainted. I didn't get a close look, but they had looked to me like gambling chits from the local racetrack. "Your sister and I have not yet really developed a routine, so I dropped by quite unannounced."

"And you read a new book to my father," Mr. Barclay said, taking a seat. I tilted my head.

"How did you know I started a new book?"

"Oh, I must have seen it on the side table when I went to visit my father this morning," he said, waving dismissively. "Did you get the opportunity to observe my sister? Are you any closer to discovering what really ails her?"

I hesitated. "She seemed very emotional again, sir. Whatever is troubling her —and I contend that I have found nothing further than her concern over her father's condition — it continues to weigh on her most heavily."

"Is that all you observed, Miss Adams?" he asked, leaning forward expectantly.

I had already decided not to discuss the glass bottle I saw in Elaine Barclay's possession until I found an opportunity to pursue that lead further myself, so I replied in the affirmative.

Barclay looked very disappointed and hung his head, his perfect curls obscuring his eyes for a moment. "You must discover the root cause of my sister's paranoia, Miss Adams. I am depending on you."

I nodded. "I know, Mr. Barclay, I truly do empathize..."

"My father worsens every single day. I am barely allowed access to him — his own son!" He ran his hands through thick auburn locks. "I feel like I am losing my entire family at once!"

I closed my eyes, feeling the burden on my shoulders driving me to speak against my better judgment. "There was one ... small thing ... that I have yet to fully explore—"

"Yes?" he demanded, dropping to his knees in front of my chair. "Anything, Miss Adams! Just give me some small drop of hope!"

I looked into his desperate eyes and could not deny him. "When your father's meal was delivered, your sister, that is Miss Barclay, she had a small glass vial in her hands ... and she was weeping."

His eyes widened and he stood slowly as if in a trance.

"I don't know what is in the vial. I had planned to discover that the next time I gained access to her rooms. I believe it is locked up in the wardrobe in the anteroom," I continued.

He was by now pacing with his back turned to me, so I stood as well.

"We need to get into that wardrobe, Mr. Barclay," I said. "Do you have a key?"

"You want to see what is in the vial because you think..." he whispered, back still turned, "you think my sister is poisoning our father with whatever is in that glass vial."

I gulped. It was a leap without information, and exactly what I had been trying to avoid. "I do not know, Mr. Barclay. I actually suspected something quite different. Nonetheless, it is just one of many unexplained things in those rooms. I would not jump to any conclusions without more data."

He turned finally, his eyes wide but determined. "But it all makes sense, don't you see? It is the guilt that has changed her, made her retreat into herself, made her bar all of us from his side! She wasn't protecting him — she was covering up her crime!"

I quickly shook my head. "I know it is tempting to take a few pieces of evidence and construct a plausible scenario, but I beg you, let us proceed with caution. We may discover that the glass vial contains something totally innocuous — like salt, for heaven's sake!"

He closed his eyes again and made a visible effort to get his emotions under control — and that was when we were startled by a brisk knock at my door.

Brian poked his head in and looked taken aback by my guest.

"Miss Adams, I just ran back to get you, but I think you had better come with us, Mr. Barclay," Dawes said, taking off his hat and opening the door wide for us to follow him out.

I picked up my coat as I said, "What is it?"

He was halfway down the stairs when he turned with an apologetic glance at my companion. "The Right Honorable Judge Barclay was pronounced dead ten minutes ago by the coroner."

CHAPTER SEVEN

The Barclay house was surrounded by police, press and curious Londoners, and even Brian struggled to get all three of us through the crowd.

James Barclay had said nothing during the ride over, and only when we had made it through his front doors did he seem to regain his tongue.

"Where is my father?" he demanded of the men in uniform gathered in his foyer.

A man I recognized well stepped forward. "You are James Barclay then, sir?" asked Sergeant Michaels.

Barclay nodded stiffly.

"Take this man to the front room," said the sergeant, directing one of his men. "Very sorry for your loss, sir, but your father is still being examined by the coroner."

I stepped forward. "Still? Is there something suspicious then about the judge's death, Sergeant?"

Sergeant Michaels looked taken aback by my presence, and then, seeing Brian, he barked, "This is not the circus, Dawes. You cannot bring friends and family to a crime scene to see the show! Most unseemly!"

Poor Brian had opened his mouth to protest but Barclay stepped in. "Apologies, Sergeant, Miss Adams is here at my behest. I had hired her to investigate something personal in my family, but in light of this," he spread his hands sadly, "I see no need to keep it a secret any longer."

"Miss Adams, you are no longer bound to secrecy," he said, putting his hand on my arm, an action that made Brian frown. "Anything you can do to aid the police, I would appreciate."

So saying, he followed the constable out of the foyer and toward his father's body.

The rest of us stood there, watching his hunched shoulders until Sergeant Michaels cleared his throat. "Hired as an investigator, eh?" He whistled. "Seems like our services aren't even required here, boys, not with Miss Adams on the case!"

I ignored his sarcasm and instead asked, "Where is Miss Barclay?"

"Locked up tight in her father's rooms," answered another officer, pointing up the stairs. "As soon as we carried Judge Barclay out of his room to the front rooms where he could be examined, she locked herself in."

I started up the stairs. "Has anything been done to bring her out?"

"No, we thought we would leave a murderer to live out her days in the comfort of her apartments," answered Sergeant Michaels, rolling his eyes. "We thought she was safe enough up there while we dealt with the body."

I turned toward him with my hand on the railing. "You've already convicted her, then?"

Sergeant Michaels crossed his beefy arms over his chest. "The doctor smelled poison on the poor man's breath as we were bringing him down the stairs. He's running some tests to confirm it now. Miss Barclay is the only one with the means, motive and opportunity to do such a thing, and in my business, that is all you need."

I looked up the stairs to where two policemen stood outside the bedroom. "Well, in my business, you also need hard evidence."

Michaels snorted.

I headed the rest of the way up the stairs, and at the bedroom door, I knocked twice. "Miss Barclay? It's Portia..."

There was silence from the other side of the door. I glanced at the officer to my left. "Is she in the bedroom or the outer room?"

He shrugged, so I turned the door handle and immediately discovered the answer to my question. For the first time since I had been in this house, the room was bathed in sunlight, the drapes spread wide, and, as I suspected, Elaine Barclay was nowhere to be seen.

Motioning for the officers to stay where they were, I looked behind me to see Brian follow me into the room, his nightstick at the ready.

He nodded encouragingly at me, so I walked over to the wardrobe and to my surprise found it open. Inside, amongst some goblets and liquor, I found a single glass vial containing some cream-colored powder. I carefully handed it to one of the officers at the door and was directing him to take it to the medical examiner when I recognized the sound of Miss Barclay weeping.

Hurriedly, I made my way over to her father's bedroom door, followed again by Brian.

"Miss Barclay," I said through the door, testing the handle. It was locked, this time from the inside. "It's me, Portia Adams."

"Go away!" she wailed.

"The police are here, Miss Barclay, you must come out," I explained. "They really must speak to you."

More wails. "I cannot! You must tell them I cannot! It is not safe!"

"Not safe?" whispered Brian at my shoulder.

"Who is not safe?" I called out.

"They didn't even let me say goodbye to him!" she cried. "And now I will never see him again!"

I absorbed that. "Your father? Of course you can see him again. Your brother is with him now. I can take you to them!"

"No, no, you can't, Portia!" she replied, hiccoughing her words through her tears. "You are not safe, none of you are!"

Brian shook his head at my questioning raised eyebrow, and then Sergeant Michaels appeared at the outer door, impatiently waving us over.

Brian holstered his weapon and automatically walked over to his superior. Spying the book I had been reading to Judge Barclay on the table, I stooped to pick it up, my senses tingling.

Odd — the bookmark I had laid in it yesterday was there, but there was something strange ... this book was newer ... the one I had been reading was dog-eared, its pages bent from someone's habit of licking their finger to turn the pages.

"Miss Adams!" Sergeant Michaels hissed at me from the doorway, but I barely heard him.

Why replace the book with a new one? And so carefully as to place the bookmark between the same pages?

Rudely ignoring the sergeant, I pushed past him and ran out of the anteroom and into the library with the book in hand. Once there, I pulled book after book off the shelves, opening them, flipping through them and tossing them aside in a frenzy. I had made it through a dozen books when the men caught up with me.

"Miss Adams, I must protest!" Sergeant Michaels said angrily, grasping my shoulder to turn me toward him.

"Help me find some dramas, please!" I said to the officers who had followed us into the room. "Plays, satires, anything like that, please!"

To my delight, and I'm sure Sergeant Michaels' consternation, all three men began scanning the bookshelves for books of that genre.

"Miss Adams, that vial you found," Sergeant Michaels said. "I need to know everything about it. James Barclay claims you have been witness to a most heinous crime!"

"I have indeed, sir," I said breathlessly, continuing to scan the bookshelves myself.

"Here!" announced one of the officers, pointing to the lowest bookshelf in the room. "All of these are dramas and plays, miss!"

He tried to hand one to me, but I raised my hands. "Please, open it?"

He looked confused but obliged me, flipping through a few pages with his gloved hand.

"Miss Adams!" Sergeant Michaels repeated, his face growing red with impatience. "We believe a man has been poisoned by his own progeny! Surely that deserves your undivided attention."

"It does." I nodded as a second officer joined the first at the lower bookshelf and started flipping through a book of collected sonnets.

"Well?" demanded Michaels as Brian entered the room, looking around at all the activity in confusion.

"Has the poison been identified?" I asked, feeling dizziness stealing over me as a third officer pulled a book from that shelf.

"Yes!" Michaels admitted. "Though a lot of good it will do poor Judge Barclay!"

"Is there an antidote at hand?" I said, reaching out to steady myself as the third book was flipped open in front of me.

Michaels looked like he was about to explode, even to my suddenly swimming vision. "Yes!" he finally burst out. "But again. The *man* is *dead!*"

"But we're not," I stated, sinking carefully onto the couch, noting the alarm on Brian's face as I pointed at the bookshelves. "Seal this room and touch nothing else till I wake."

"Till you wake?" asked Brian, who was looking very blurry to me, even as he stepped closer.

"And administer the antidote to Miss Barclay and then myself immediately," I managed to say before giving in to the darkness.

I awoke on the settee I had selected for myself in the same room, with Dr. Joyce and Brian bent over me. Both heaved sighs as my eyes focused first on the doctor where he crouched beside the settee, and then on Brian, who was hovering over him. "Welcome back," the doctor said with a smile.

"Thank you, Doctor," I said, slowly sitting up with the doctor's help. "How long was I out?"

"Less than fifteen minutes, because you knew your own ailment," replied the doctor, replacing his equipment in his bag. "If only I had known that Marcus was being poisoned with cyanide, I could have cured him as easily and as well, poor man! In small amounts, this particular poison works over time, though you might have a more delicate constitution, Miss Adams, as it affected you quite dramatically. I have administered amyl nitrite now, but you should rest here until you feel better."

Brian sat down beside me on the couch and wrapped an arm around my shoulders just as Sergeant Michaels and James Barclay entered the library.

"How did you manage to get yourself poisoned, Adams?" Sergeant Michaels demanded.

"The same way Marcus Barclay did, sir," I said, looking at James Barclay, feeling Brian's arm stiffen around me. "And the same way poor Elaine Barclay did."

Barclay looked decidedly worried, and when he glanced around the room at the books strewn everywhere, he seemed to pale even more.

"Judge Barclay's food was poisoned by his own child, that much is clear, but how did you and Elaine Barclay come to get poisoned?" Michaels said. "Did she make a mistake? Or did she realize that you saw her administering the poison and somehow poison you as well?"

"It was a mistake, one the killer tried to correct," I said, "because they needed me very much alive."

I tried to stand and pace but didn't quite have my balance back yet, so I sat back down next to Brian. "The books you see all over the floor — if you examine them, you will see that each has been meticulously poisoned," I explained, pointing at the books littering the floor. "All except the plays — the Shakespeare, the Henry James, the Greek tragedies — those are untouched."

"Poisoned?" repeated Michaels. "How do you poison a book?"

"By applying a liquefied version of the poison to the tops of the pages with a brush, I suspect," I suggested. "If you knew that your intended victim had the habit of licking their finger and turning the page, it would be a reasonable way to deliver poison."

"A reasonable way to..." Sergeant Michaels repeated again. "We already have a 'reasonable' way, Miss Adams. Judge Barclay's food was being poisoned by his daughter, using that very glass vial that you identified!"

"Yes, that is what I was meant to discover, was it not, Mr. Barclay?" I said, looking at my classmate. "You hired me as an unwitting accomplice to help frame your sister for murder."

The room went silent at my words, Sergeant Michaels looking back and forth between us, Dr. Joyce and the other officers looking shocked, but I had eyes only for James Barclay. Brian stood up and stalked over to the man's side, taking hold of his upper arm.

"Answer Miss Adams," he commanded, his lip curled in an expression I had never seen before.

Barclay said nothing, only stood there, as if in shock.

"But," said Dr. Joyce, "it was Elaine Barclay who barred my colleagues and I from examining her father, not James. If not for Elaine, one of us would have discovered that the man was being poisoned, and we could have saved Marcus's life!"

"Yes, and when Miss Barclay is made aware of that, it will likely haunt her for the rest of her life," I admitted. "But her crime was gullibility, influenced by her brother's actions, and fear brought on by months of poisoning. Not premeditated murder."

I glanced again at James Barclay, but he remained silent, even with Brian and now Sergeant Michaels looking at him with accusing eyes.

"I will admit that this plan was very bold, but if you examine these books, you will find the evidence I described. I have never taken a meal or even a drink in this house. These books were the only opportunity to poison me, and I contend it was a mistake. If you will allow me to at least demonstrate Miss Barclay's innocence, I will make an attempt," I said, standing finally.

Sergeant Michaels had opened his mouth, probably to deny me, but Constable Dawes spoke up. "If you could coax Miss Barclay out of her rooms without violence, that would be helpful to us, Miss Adams."

He winked at me from behind the sergeant's back, though not in amusement. I could see how hard he was gripping Barclay's arm, and when Michaels whirled to glare at him, I winked back. Michaels instructed the two other officers to hold James Barclay in this room, and then followed my lead with Dr. Joyce and Brian in tow. We stopped at the door, where I whispered in Brian's ear and he nodded.

I re-entered the anteroom and proceeded straight to the locked door as Dawes pulled closed all the drapes in the room.

"Are you sure you know what you are doing?" whispered Brian as he returned to my side, his words for my ears only.

"No," was my unreassuring whispered response.

I knocked on the door. "Miss Barclay, it is Portia again. We have brought your father's body back up here so that you can say goodbye."

"Impossible! No, Portia! No tricks! I will not come out!" she said from her side of the door. "My brother was here a few moments ago, and he admitted that he hired you to spy on me! I know it all now!"

I gritted my teeth and would have glared at James Barclay had he had the temerity to follow me in here. "Miss Barclay, at the very least, you must take this antidote from Dr. Joyce. You and I have been poisoned, just like your father ... please let us in?"

Silence from the other side of the door, then: "Another trick, Portia? There was no poison! I saw to all my father's meals, I ate the same food, there was no poison!"

"Miss Barclay, I assure you Miss Adams was poisoned. I administered an antidote to her not a half-hour ago," Dr. Joyce called out. "If this is also what ails you, I beg you to let me treat you, child!"

Miss Barclay began to cry again at his entreaties, and my heart went out to her.

"You cannot cure me, doctor, no more than you could my father," she said through her tears. "I tried to treat us both. I tried to keep all of you safe..."

Suddenly I felt another click in my brain and wondered if perhaps ... no ... it was too simple ... and too far-fetched ... wasn't it?

Sergeant Michaels was straightening his tie, a sign that he had given up on this verbal negotiation and had already decided on a more aggressive course of action.

"Miss Barclay," I said through the door, following my instinct, no matter how implausible. "The small glass vial I saw you applying to your father's food, what was in it?"

Silence from the other side of the door.

"Was it garlic powder, Miss Barclay?" I asked, and was answered immediately by a loud gasp from her side of the door.

"Garlic powder?" repeated Dr. Joyce.

"Sunlight, garlic, burns in daylight, pale skin and blood on the lips," I listed, and saw a spark of understanding come into Brian's eyes.

I smiled and whispered to Michaels, and then turned back to the door. "We are going to leave, Miss Barclay. Your father's body is here on your bed, and I've closed all the drapes again. Please come out and say your goodbyes at least."

I then directed the men to hide behind the drapes in the total darkness and closed the outer door, slipping behind the drapes where Dawes hid.

Minutes went by and I began to fear that Elaine Barclay's paranoia could not allow her to trust me, when finally she peeked out the door hesitantly. Seeing the room exactly as I had told her it would be, she blindly rushed to the bed where Michaels lay and was seized.

Elaine screamed as she was grabbed, and we whipped open the drapes to see her struggling for her life with the man who held her captive.

She twisted her head toward me, red-rimmed eyes accusing. "You have killed me, Portia Adams!"
"No." I sadly shook my head, feeling none of the triumph I should. "I have not, Miss Barclay, I swear. Look at yourself. You do not burn in the sunlight. You remain, like any of us, whole and unscathed!"

"Well, of course she remains!" Sergeant Michaels said, almost losing his grip as his struggling victim stopped moving suddenly.

Hesitantly, Elaine Barclay looked up into the sunlight streaming into the room, squinting with wonder. The bags under her eyes were so pronounced and purple that she looked as though she had been boxing with Bruiser Jenkins. The skin was stretched tight over her cheekbones and she had taken to biting her lips so much that tiny scars could be seen on that delicate skin.

"Please, take this antidote from Dr. Joyce, Elaine," I said as kindly as I could. "And I swear, I will explain everything."

"Explain it to me first, Adams," Sergeant Michaels ordered as we stood aside for Dr. Joyce to do his work.

I sighed but nodded. "I believe that if you look into James Barclay's finances, you will find a man who is heavily in debt despite his inheritance, because of habits that promise only more debt, not less. You will also find a man who stood at odds with his highly successful father, and whose leanings towards the theater and gambling caused a great deal of tension in this household."

"Exactly true, Miss Adams," admitted Dr. Joyce as he stood. "But Marcus was a very proud, very private man, so how did you discover all this?"

"My first conversation with James Barclay told me his ambitions were not toward law, but toward performance and acting, and then the placement of his books in the family library — at the very lowest level, hidden almost — speaks of where his interests lay in the hierarchy of his father's support."

Michaels gestured for me to continue.

"I am guessing that James Barclay's habits and Judge Barclay's tolerance of them came to a head within the last year, resulting in James conceiving of this plan," I said, pacing. "His father would never accept his lifestyle, but James needed his financial support, if not emotional, so the poor man was marked for death. But as a younger sibling, his elder sister and her husband would inherit, and James would simply be trading like-minded masters — for Mr. Ridley and Miss Barclay seem much more like Judge Barclay in sensibility than like James."

Dr. Joyce nodded again, passing Elaine a glass of water.

"So the plan had to be extended to include framing the sister and ending the engagement," I said, chewing my lip thoughtfully. "By then, I believe James had already decided to use poison. And that he had chosen a poison that could be administered slowly through the method I have already described."

"Knowing his father's and his sister's shared taste in books, and that they shared the habit of licking their finger to turn pages, his plan was simple. He would poison all the books in the family library except his. They never even looked at that poor bookshelf where his precious plays were condemned, and he could sit amongst them, reading his own books while they poisoned themselves.

"He watched them sicken, night after night, licking their fingers as they turned page after fatal page," I described, seeing the scene in my mind's eye. "He knew that his father read far more than his sister, it being part of his job reviewing case law, and he also knew that one of the side effects of this particular poison was a slow descent into paranoia and hallucinations — a most helpful symptom for his purposes."

"To what end?" Sergeant Michaels asked, his brow furrowed, but looking decidedly less angry.

"To convince Miss Barclay that she and her father had somehow been infected by vampirism," I answered.

Brian spoke up then. "It's why the drapes were always drawn, why you ended your engagement, why you locked the doors and stopped going outside, is it not, Miss Barclay?"

She looked up from her seat, and already the hectic look in her eyes had receded. "It all seems too fantastical now, I know, but all the signs were there! My brother started reading *Dracula* to my father when he first fell ill, and the more he read, the more I feared!"

I nodded, encouraging her.

"One morning, about a month after my father fell ill, and a week after I started to feel a little weak myself, I found ... a mouse." She shuddered. "It was drained of blood ... and on my father's lips...

Oh, dear God, how that scared me! I told James about it directly, and he assured me it was just a story and threw the mouse away!

"But then, two weeks later, my father and I were on our way to Dr. Joyce's office when, I swear, his skin started to burn before our very eyes!" she said, tears streaming down her cheeks again. "Mr. Ridley was with us, and he too ... he did not think it very important, but I made him take us straight home, and that was the last time I let my father out into the daylight!"

"Your brother probably applied some kind of salve that was sensitive to light, Elaine," I explained. "Perhaps some highly concentrated kerosene mixed with his hand cream?"

"But why did you not speak of it to us, child? Or to Mr. Ridley?" Dr. Joyce exclaimed.

Elaine Barclay shook her head, so I answered for her. "Because in her extreme paranoia, doctor, caused by and fed daily by her brother, she thought she was protecting all of us from the monsters she and her father had become."

CHAPTER EIGHT

B ut I don't understand," I said to Brian as we walked his dogs a few mornings later, taking a route through Regent's Park, "how can all of your leads have dried up?"

It was the first time I had been out of my apartment in days, only coaxed out by Brian's promise of an update on our pursuit of Sherlock Holmes.

He stooped to pick up some of the yellow leaves that had fallen and threw them before answering. The musty smell of fall permeated the cool air around us. "The officer who served under Inspector Lestrade, who sought Holmes out when he was keeping bees in the countryside — he's not returning my calls anymore. I'm going to stop by his house tomorrow in Westminster."

"Interesting," I replied, uncoiling the leashes as the dogs crossed each other's paths. "You remember those society pages we found in *The Daily*'s archives with a few photos and mentions of my grandmother's attendance in the captions beneath?"

Brian nodded, so I continued. "Well, I managed to get copies of the images, but the photographers are both long dead, and the page is identified as having been written by 'Staff of *The Daily*,' so there's nothing at the end of that lead either."

I pulled an envelope from my shoulder bag and in flipping through it passed over the two photos I was speaking of. The photos were composites, with several images in square boxes, a headline above and the article below. They were slightly blurry images, being almost fifty years old, but you could easily make out dancing couples in large ballrooms, a pair of women in gloves and feathered hats toasting champagne glasses with a man in a top hat and a caption beneath identifying some of the subjects.

"The Earl of Shrewsbury raises a glass with renowned opera singer Irene Adler in attendance," Brian read from one of the photos, turning wide eyes my way. "Is that not the same Irene Adler..."

"I believe so, from the casebook Watson called "A Scandal in Bohemia"," I answered with a rueful smile. "She certainly ran in the highest circles."

"As did your grandmother. Look at her here," Brian replied, pointing to a photo identified as 'Socialite Constance Adams takes a turn around the dance floor with the Earl of Effingham'.

I took the photo from his hands to look again as he reached down to untwist the dogs' leashes for the third time on this walk. With a frown, I realized Irene Adler was also in this shot, in profile, standing along the edge of the dancers near a window in the hall.

With a start I felt a flash of recognition at that profile, at the nose and jaw, and even in the posture of the woman in the image. I raised my eyes from the photo, thinking about the casebook and notes back in my apartment. Adler was American, an opera singer, and a contemporary of my grandparents and my guardian. She was also a brilliant criminal — one of the very few to have escaped Holmes and Watson.

Brian reached down to pick up a stick and throw it. The three dogs watched the stick as it arced through the air all the way to where it hit the ground, and then they all looked expectantly back at Brian.

With perfect timing, he shrugged and said, "I wasn't even throwing it for you scamps. It's how I stay so fit. Throw a stick, pick it up ... you know."

I gave a tiny smile at his joke as he went to retrieve the stick and quickly returned to my side, his long legs making short work of the distance.

We walked in silence for a moment, my thoughts a thousand miles away, and then he said, "It still bothers you, doesn't it ... how close Barclay came to getting away with murder?"

I clenched my jaw, staring straight ahead.

"It's all right to be bothered," he continued, throwing the stick again and getting the same response from the dogs. "But you have to know that he would have gotten away with it had you not figured out his motives and methodologies. You are why James Barclay is sitting in a jail cell while his sister recovers in hospital."

"I am also why Judge Barclay is not with his daughter on the same floor, but in the morgue three levels down," I replied, for the first time voicing aloud why I had been sullen and withdrawn since solving the case.

"Now," he said, stopping to turn toward me, forcing me to do the same or trip on middle-aged dogs, "James Barclay killed the judge. No one else is to blame for that heinous murder but the son."

"But ... he hired me to be his accomplice," I replied, looking down at my gloved hands, determined not to cry. "And he escalated his timeline when he poisoned me by mistake and..."

Brian put both his hands on my forearms, and even through his gloves and my coat I could feel the warmth radiating from them. "If you had never been hired, if you had never gone into that house, would Mr. Barclay have ceased his murderous plan? Would he have given up trying to kill his father and frame his sister?"

I shook my head, having drawn the same conclusion over sleepless nights. No, the man had spent months devising and implementing this plan. He was determined to kill his father and take his money.

"Then what you have done is thwarted a villain who was stupid enough to underestimate you," he said, using his gloved right hand to raise my chin so my eyes met his. "Forget James Barclay. Focus on your accomplishment."

"*Our* accomplishment," I answered with a lopsided smile, still thinking about Adler and deciding this was not the right time to bring my startling suspicions before Brian.

He laughed, dropping his arms and resuming his forward motion. "Fine then, our accomplishment, though the act I am most proud of is not punching the blighter in the nose in front of my sergeant."

We walked another few meters in silence, and then Brian asked, "So, was that all you found out?"

"Pardon?"

"You said that you had 'almost' no luck," he reminded me. "That implies that you had at least a little..."

"Oh, yes, one reporter at *The Sunday Times* claims to have spoken to Sherlock Holmes at Watson's funeral," I replied, nodding at Brian's surprise before continuing. "His name is Richard Graft, and after finally convincing him that I wasn't a competing reporter, he admitted that he had attended the funeral with that express ambition, sure that Watson's old partner would attend. He says Holmes did attend, standing as far back from the group as possible, and was very rude when approached."

"So far that sounds accurate of what you and I know of Holmes' character," Brian replied, back at my side, and turning us, dogs and all, back toward home.

"It does, and what's more, the reporter had photographs," I said, replacing the photos from the society pages in the envelope and pulling out the others.

We stopped again, this time at a handy wrought iron and wood bench, to pass five photos back and forth. The first two were panoramic and taken from afar of the full group that attended the funeral, with many attendees in uniform — police and military. Several women could also be seen in the front row of the gravesite, clothed all in black. I squinted at the women and identified one as potentially having the same build and posture as Adler. The next photo seemed to be taken from the same vantage point since you could see the edge of the group on its far right, with an empty space of gravestones and sparse trees in the center and then a lonely figure behind a tree on the far left of the image.

The final two images were of this lonely figure, one more taken a little closer, and the last taken at a distance where the subject must have been aware of the photographer and had turned his face away from the camera.

Brian held this one in his hands when he said, "So this a recent photo our elusive Mr. Holmes." He whistled under his breath. "Did this Graft fellow get any information about where Holmes was living or traveling?"

"When pressed at the time, Holmes claimed to be traveling abroad," I answered, taking back the photos and carefully putting them in the envelope.

"Europe?" asked Brian, resuming our walk and leading us out of the park.

"No," I replied, cocking my head to see his reaction. "Interestingly enough, Canada."

CHAPTER NINE

Two days later, I sat with Mrs. Jones in front of my fireplace. I had just explained this latest case, and she was still full to the brim with questions.

"But why involve you at all, Portia?" she said, leaning forward to pour a bit more tea into both our cups.

"Hmm?" I replied, my brain and eyes focused on studying her profile, comparing it with Irene Adler's. "Sorry, why involve me?"

She nodded, eyeing me curiously.

"I think things were not progressing fast enough for Mr. Barclay's debtors," I suggested with a nod of thanks. "No one had yet accused Elaine Barclay of anything, his father had still not died despite months of poisoning, and if he died without any doubt being cast on the daughter then Barclay would have only accomplished half his goal. And two suspicious deaths by poisoning were out of the question, so he needed to resolve this problem quickly.

"He knew of my background and assumed I had enough skill to follow the trail he laid, and that I had enough credibility with the Yard to bring them along as well. And by hiring me to help 'save' his sister, he could have a witness to his shock and outrage when her evil plan was revealed."

My guardian shook her head. "He underestimated you, little one."

I nodded. "And I him. I was taken in by his charms, and he truly has a talent for acting that I fear will continue to go unappreciated where he is going. If it had not been for my accidental poisoning, I might not have made the connection at all."

"How did that happen? You would think he would have been very careful for your sake and his to not mix up the poisoned and unpoisoned books," my guardian remarked.

"Oh, he was careful. He picked the book I was to read to Mr. Barclay — one of his plays, and therefore unpoisoned. A very long book that would take me several weeks to finish reading aloud. I am sure it was his intention that it be the only book I handled during my unwitting support of his plan. It was only on the day that I dropped by unannounced that I got hold of a poisoned book by mistake."

"When he realized his mistake, he rushed me over here and had you wash away all the evidence from my hands and skin," I explained. "He knew that the risk of my discovering his plan had suddenly trebled by poisoning me, so he left to enact the final stage of his murder."

"The vial?" she asked, brow arched.

"The vial," I agreed. "He knew all about it, knew it contained ground garlic, and had a key to the wardrobe. He filled the contents of the vial with powdered cyanide and allowed his poor sister to administer the final murderous act."

"And then, when he came by the next day to check on you, he bullied you into seeing his planted clues," she said, eyeing me carefully.

"Indeed. He must have known that his father's death was imminent, within a few meals at most, so he needed to push me toward the correct conclusion immediately. I wondered why he looked so nervous but wrongfully assumed it was his concern for me that made his state of dress so out of character," I said, stirring a slice of lemon into my tea. "He needed me to reveal my findings in front of the police at his house. Everyone would believe Elaine Barclay was the murderer. She would be almost incoherent in her paranoid state, and James Barclay would inherit all."

"And you would have been an accessory to his dark deeds. He would never have considered making you a part of his plan had you not been the heir to the most famous detective offices in the world," my guardian said. "Are you finally seeing the terrible burden this house seems to lay on you? Do you really want to add to that by associating yourself with Sherlock Holmes directly?"

I thoughtfully sipped at my tea and found nothing to say.

UNFOUND: Casebook 3

London, Christmas, 1930

Oh dear!" fussed Mrs. Dawes as she fluttered around me. "You're going to miss your train, I just know it, and then what will we say to Mrs. Jones?"

I shook my head fondly at her as I watched her son pick up my valise and start in surprise at its weight. He was wearing a forest green sweater that seemed to complement his eyes and skin color in a way that distracted me from the conversation every time I looked directly at him.

Thankfully, turning my eyes just a little from the Dawes presented my garishly decorated townhouse instead. Mrs. Dawes had assured me that she and our neighbor, Mrs. Katz, decorated the outside of their townhouses every year, and it being of no importance to me and seemingly of much importance to her, I agreed to her continued leadership on the matter.

It wasn't that the garlands and bells weren't festive, it was that no color had been left unexplored, making it a chaotic eyesore — at least to my eyes. My mother had celebrated Christmas, decorating the house mostly with handmade doilies and strings of popcorn, and perhaps she was the one to blame for my spartan decorating tastes.

"I would never presume to advise a lady on her packing," Brian said, carefully hauling the valise out the door. "But surely you could do without the marble sink that you have in here?"

I caught his eye and smiled. Brian knew me well enough to guess at the contents of my suitcase — and it wasn't a marble sink.

"There are only eight casebooks in there," I defended myself as his mother continued to cluck around me in a distracting orbit.

"Harrumph!" he said, getting my luggage into the hackney. "A little light reading, then? You are supposed to be relaxing in Edinburgh, are you not?"

"Yes, of course," I agreed as his mother dashed up to my rooms. "But knowing ... Mrs. Jones as I do, I anticipate that despite her best intentions, I will be left with swaths of time to fill on my own. What better use of my time than to familiarize myself with the techniques of comparing victims of suicide and of homicide?"

"And what about our search for Sherlock Holmes?" he said, looking around to make sure we were alone. "You haven't talked about your progress on that front in weeks. And now you're going away..."

I shrugged, trying to seem nonchalant, but the truth was, since finding that photo of Irene Adler with my grandmother Constance Adams at a society ball almost fifty years ago, I had refocused my research on Adler instead. The introduction of Bruiser Jenkins and their decades-old friendship had added fuel to the fire, taking me back to the archived society pages again and again. Several of the notebooks in my valise were actually filled with details the press had written about Irene Adler's exploits and marriages.

I had not yet shared my findings with Brian, well aware of his commitment to Scotland Yard and unsure if I could ask him to keep a secret like this. And more and more it was looking like this was a reality, not just my suspicions. My bag was packed with casebooks and all the evidence I had managed to gather — from the old posters from concert halls featuring photos of Adler in her operatic costumes to the notes I had made comparing the timeline of Adler's and Jones's lives. I suspected far more than a simple change of name to disguise past criminal activity. I thought I might have uncovered the real reason why my mother had left me in the care of this woman, and why *the woman*, as Holmes had referred to her, had accepted such a responsibility.

I was taking it all with me to confront her with it far away as possible from Baker Street and Brian Dawes. I glanced at him again and forced my thoughts away from that unpleasant confrontation.

"I got you something, nothing really, just ... something," I said, pulling a small package out of my pocket and pressing it into his hands.

"What a coincidence, since, well, would you look at that!" He pulled something of about the same size and shape from his trouser pocket. "I have something small for you as well!"

We laughed, exchanging the gifts and then glancing at each other for permission to open them. When we both nodded and laughed again, I pulled off my gloves and made to unwrap the cloth-wrapped gift.

Brian had gone the more direct route, pulling the brown paper off in one handful and holding his present up to his eye. "A magnifying glass?" He laughed again. "Both elegant and useful, thank you!"

"And it has several magnifications," I explained excitedly. "They fold behind each other into the leather case so you can use them as you need them. Also, there is a clip to attach it to your uniform belt."

"I see that," he replied, his grin wide and his dimples deep. "Thank you!"

"You are so welcome," I replied, glad he liked it because I had agonized over his gift. Meanwhile, I had pulled the ribbon off the cloth, and on unwrapping it discovered that it was the gift itself, folded inside out and tied up.

"It's a print of old London from ..." I said, shaking it out to see it better, and found the corner with the date of printing. "From 1885?"

"It's how Holmes and Watson saw the world when they lived here," he explained, clipping the magnifying glass onto his belt to take the other two corners so that the cloth was held between us like a picnic blanket we were about to lay on the ground.

"It's ... I really don't know what to say," I said, thrilled with this gift and the fact that I had a friend who knew me so well. "It's perfect. I can't wait to hang it up in my room. I think I'll put it right above my bed so I can look up at it when I am lying down!"

Brian waggled his eyebrows, and that was a little suggestive. I blushed and cleared my throat.

We stood on the sidewalk a trifle awkwardly, me folding up the cloth map and then adjusting the light satchel over my shoulder, and Brian shifting from foot to foot until I extended my hand, which he readily shook.

"Happy Christmas," he said. "And try to shake off this last case, would you? Anyone else would be thrilled with the result of capturing a murderer. Lord knows Sergeant Michaels can't stop talking about it — mentioning your name as little as possible, by the way."

I tried to smile, but the memory of how close I came to accusing an innocent woman of murder — on behalf of the actual murderer, of all people — was still too close and I had not quite recovered my usual level of confidence. Instead I nodded at my friend as his mother re-emerged with a warm bonnet from the two-story townhouse we all shared.

"I will promise to try if you promise to leave some crimes unsolved for me until after the holidays when I return," I said, giving his mother a hug and wishing her a Happy Christmas before stepping into the cab, bonnet in hand, and speeding on my way with a wave.

CHAPTER TWO

The *Flying Scotsman*, as it had been famously dubbed, left promptly at ten o'clock every morning from King's Cross Station. Despite my calm when compared to Mrs. Dawes' frenzy, when I got out of my cab the clock outside the station forced me to hasten.

The smells of the hundreds of Londoners who frequented this station every day assaulted my nose as soon as I closed the cab door, but the sight of begging children, hurried businessmen, families with huge trunks of luggage and the madness of the rush was a lot to take in all at the same time. I reminded myself to visit this station at an off-peak time, the better to observe it.

The volume of voices combined with train whistles and announcements on the loudspeaker made it hard, but I finally got the attention of a porter, and with his cart, we sprinted to my destination: Platform 10. I had the tip ready so that my valise was transferred rapidly from porter to luggage handler and I was on board the train with moments to spare.

I was, of course, not the only late arrival as whistles sounded the final boarding call. As I made my way to the compartment my first-class ticket had paid for, I could see several other would-be passengers through the windows of the train making the same dash.

I was stopped by one of the conductors, who perused my ticket wearing eyeglasses that were obviously not adequate for his failing eyesight. As I waited patiently, a young woman leading a small blonde child by the hand pushed through the crowd on the platform. They ran past and out of my sight toward first class.

I glanced at my conductor, but he was still struggling and a line-up was forming behind me, so I said, "Can I help you, sir? The numbers are AA12..."

"Yes, yes," he mumbled and handed back my ticket, to repeat the process on the poor individual behind me. I took the ticket and continued on my way with a sigh, checking the numbers on the compartment doors as I went.

My very rich, highly secretive guardian had arranged this private compartment for my trip to meet her, and sliding open the glassed door, I felt trepidation at the prospect of what awaited me when I disembarked. I knew what I had to do when I got to Edinburgh, but the idea of confronting my guardian with the knowledge that she was in fact Irene Adler, adversary of my own grandfather and unexplainably good friends with my grandmother Constance Adams, took my stress up to a new level. How had they traveled in the same circles? How was it possible that Constance Adams, married to Dr. Watson, had also been friends with Irene Adler?

At the end of the casebook involving Adler, she had disappeared from Watson and Holmes's life — at least according to the notebooks. There was no other mention of her except as the only woman to have bested Holmes. It seemed obvious that Adler and Constance had remained friends after my grandmother left Watson, even attending his funeral after her friend's death. All of this meant that I felt more than a little twinge of guilt when enjoying the fruits of her crimes, like this trip.

The compartment was made up of two long benches that looked more like expensive couches except for their wooden backs that made up the walls on either side. There was a large curtained window between them, the lower pane slightly raised. In addition to the compartment door, there were long drapes tied up on either side of the glass door, so I loosened the golden cords that held them in place, allowing their thick fabric to cover the doorway. Now it looked like I was ensconced in a brocade nook, the fabric of the couches complementing the drapes and even the walls of the compartment in burgundies and yellows.

Out my window I saw another woman and child run in the opposite direction toward third class as the train jerked to a start. Removing yesterday's newspaper, I pushed my satchel onto the luggage shelf above the bench seat. My valise may have been heavy with casebooks, but I restricted myself to my new notebook for this adventure, along with a small wallet.

Several throw pillows were stacked on one side of the bench seat, so I chose that one to arrange myself on, propping my back up comfortably to look out the window so I could watch our progress out of the train yard. The whistle sounded again as we gained speed, the rhythmic pattern of the wheels passing over tracks speeding up as well. To the north, it was easy to see the hills of Hampstead and Highgate, and the snowy blanket only heightened their mysterious beauty.

With college out for the season, I had been quietly dreading spending the holidays alone in my apartment at 221B Baker Street. The holidays were a time for family, after all, and it made me miss my dear departed mother even more than usual.

I had spent a total of five evenings with the brothers Watson and their large families, and despite enjoying being a part of a family again, the raucousness of the many children and the multitude of questions about Canada and San Francisco and the cases I was working on were tiring. I had just wrapped up a case that had, more than anything else, damaged my ability to trust. And then so quickly on its heels I had made the connection between Irene Adler and Irene Jones — which felt like a second blow to my ability to trust. Finally, my suspicions about Adler's true relationship to me, and my mother's knowledge of that — that was the third and final blow. Was no one who they seemed? How could I trust anyone?

Therefore, when my rather excitable guardian had invited me to visit her at her home in Edinburgh (one of many she held all over the world), I determinedly accepted the offer, unwilling to let this fester any longer.

The rocking of the train and the pristine white of the landscape had the expected effect of relaxing me. But only minutes had passed in this serene state when I was jerked fully awake by a woman's scream. I sat up straight, cocking my ear for either a repeat of the sound or a signal that I had mistaken it for something else — a train whistle, perhaps. Several more minutes passed, and I watched some official-looking men run past my compartment toward the front of the train. A few minutes later, a group of men headed in the opposite direction, passed by more men heading the same way as the first group.

My curiosity never really needed much to arouse it, so I slid open my door just as a conductor, followed by a constable, passed by me in a rush.

I waited a beat and then followed them down the hallway. Only five compartments away, still in first class, a small party of people was gathered around a door through which a woman's sobs could easily be heard.

"But what could have happened to her?" a passenger whispered to her companion.

"Happened to whom?" I asked, trying to see into the compartment.

"Why, to the child of course!" the second woman said excitedly.

Another fit of sobs brought our attention back to the compartment, and that was when the constable reappeared at the doorway.

"All o' ye need tae get back to your seats," he announced in a thick Scottish accent. "Leave us to our business. Go on now!"

CHAPTER THREE

He waved his large hands at the crowd as if trying to disperse flies buzzing around a meal. He was tall, with rounded shoulders, a bit of a pot belly, a long graying mustache and deep wrinkles about his eyes.

He also had a scowl that would make even Mrs. Jones take a step back, so, grumbling and whispering, the various passengers did as they were told and ebbed around me until I stood alone in the passageway.

I would like to say that I fought hard to mind my own business, but, I rationalized, mysteries were my business, so...

I stepped closer to the open door and stuck my head in as unobtrusively as possible. "Please, can I help in any way? Perhaps I could fetch a glass of water or a blanket?"

I used those precious seconds to take a mental photograph of the scene in that compartment. A young woman of under thirty sat cradling her head. A huge welt was even now beginning to purple around her weeping eye. The left side of her face was swollen from the blow that had caused that welt, her blonde hair in disarray, half matted to the side of her head and the other half hanging limply on her shoulder. The pot-bellied constable, who had been taking notes, turned toward me with his right hand on his baton. I judged him to be about forty — a little old to still be a constable, but obviously at the ready. The only other occupant of the compartment was an older man in his sixties who was patting the woman's hand in a comforting way.

"Here now! You've been telt already tae clear off!" the constable barked at me.

"You did, sir, I admit," I replied, holding my ground. "I only sought to offer my aid."
"Why don't you sit down here, miss, and keep Mrs. Anderson company while I run and get her that water?" suggested the kindly older man. And without waiting for anyone's approval, he bustled out of the compartment.

I took advantage of his quick decision and sat down next to the woman.

"Why don't you continue, sir? I promise not to cause trouble," I said.

The officer must have seen that I meant no harm, because he mumbled "Americans" under his breath but resumed his questioning.

"I've got Borgins and Jameson searching right now, Mrs. Anderson, but I want tae get every detail from ye. Ye say ye were struck down in this very compartment in the presence of your daughter, Leah?" he said.

Mrs. Anderson nodded weakly, and then winced at the pain that caused her.

"D'ye ken if there was anyone else in the hallway?" he asked.

"No," she whispered.

"And when ye woke, through Mr. James Arnold's discovery of ye, lying on the floor here, your wee bairn was gone," the constable continued.

"Yes!" wailed poor Mrs. Anderson. "Please, let us stop going over the story again and again, and find Leah!"

The constable raised his hands. "I swear, all is being done to find her, Mrs. Anderson, but I must ken one more thing: when ye were attacked, was the train in motion or were we still stopped on the platform?"

"We were moving, sir," the gentleman identified as Mr. Arnold answered, re-entering the compartment bearing the promised glass of water. "I had just introduced myself to Mrs. Anderson and her daughter Leah as we left the station. And then I left to check on some friends in the next compartment, and when I got back..." He handed the glass of water to Mrs. Anderson, patting her hand. "I am so sorry I wasn't here to stop this from happening, my dear!"

She sniffed tearfully up at him and took the glass of water in her shaking hands.

"How long do you estimate you were gone?" I couldn't help but ask.

Mr. Arnold looked surprised, but answered, "Why, maybe ten minutes..."

"And did you pass anyone in the hallway — either on the way out or on the way back in?"

"I already asked that of them, miss, and Mr. Arnold telt me he did not," the constable broke in, a little annoyed with my questions.

"Then where is she?" demanded Mrs. Anderson, trying to stand but failing.

"Your bairn is still on board this train, m'um, don't you fash yourself — and I will find her!" the constable replied. "This here is a non-stop trip, dinnae ye ken? No one can get off or on for eight hours."

"That's right," agreed Mr. Arnold reassuringly. "There's already a band of constables out there looking. I passed them on the way back from the dining car. They'll find Leah in no time!"

"I heard there was need for a doctor?" came a new voice from the doorway. "My name is Dr. Ewing," said a tall man, carrying a medical bag.

"Ah, yes, sir, if ye could see to Mrs. Anderson's injuries, I must consult with my men," the constable said, rising and nodding at Arnold and I to do the same.

I patted Mrs. Anderson awkwardly on the arm and followed the men back into the hallway, where the constable slid the door closed behind us, leaving the doctor with his patient.

"Now, we are working with a description of the wee bairn given tae us by the conductor who seated them, but I'd like tae hear it from ye as well, sir," the constable said, licking the tip of his pencil and holding it expectantly over his notebook.

"Young, around six or seven, I'd estimate, blonde with ringlets, all the way down over her shoulders," described Arnold, pressing his thumb and forefinger to his temple. "She was wearing a pink dress that matched her pink jacket — that was left behind in the compartment ... and she had a birthmark — a red one, on her cheek — about the size of a ha'penny."

The constable checked all of this against his existing notes and nodded. "The birthmark was mentioned by the conductor as well, as was her bright blonde hair."

The doctor slid open the door and stepped out into the hallway. "I would like to give Mrs. Anderson a mild sedative to help alleviate the shock and allow me to treat her cheek. I fear she might have a fracture," he explained, "but she insists on not being alone, and asks for your attention, sir."

He said this last to Mr. Arnold, who of course agreed, and they re-entered the cabin, leaving the constable and me in the hallway.

"You should return to your seat, miss...?" the constable suggested.

"Portia Adams," I replied, and then threw in, "of Baker Street. And you are?"

"Constable Perkins," he answered automatically, not placing my famous address, or perhaps not caring. He tipped his hat. "I must catch up with my men now."

So saying, he hurried toward the front of the train. He was right, of course; the train had been in motion since the assault and abduction, so the child was still on board, hopefully safe, but surely distraught after seeing her mother knocked unconscious.

CHAPTER FOUR

A struggling, screaming child should not be hard to find in such a confined area," I mused aloud, heading back toward my compartment.

I slid the door open and resumed my seat next to the window, picking up my discarded newspaper from the floor. *What a risky way to kidnap a child!* I thought. Surely not a well-thought-out plan, with no escape for eight hours? Perhaps the kidnapper had thought to get off the train before it left the station, and something went wrong?

I shook my head, folding the newspaper, and then, reaching up to put it in my satchel, I pulled out my notebook and pencil instead. I sat back down to detail the case.

An hour at least passed in this fashion, and twice I was interrupted by a group of men who knocked, asked to search my compartment and were granted full access.

The second time, I had to ask how the search progressed.

"Not well, miss," a young conductor admitted, wiping his brow. "This is our second sweep, and so far, no hint of the little girl."

"No one saw or heard anything at all?" I asked incredulously. "Surely someone heard the child's screams? Witnessed a struggle? Even one that was explained away as an unruly tantrum?"

The man shook his head sadly as the troupe wrapped up its physical search and the men tipped their hats to me.
I stood for a moment, unable to settle back down, and then decisively headed to the dining compartment, notebook in hand. It had more of the same brocade found in my compartment on the seat pads and in the wallpaper that marked this car. The drapes in here were the burgundy rather than the gold, and were all open, affording the diners views of the passing scenery. More than twenty tables for four were arranged in various positions around this car, with a bar in the northeastern corner of the room and waiters in pristine white uniforms moving quickly from table to table. The

mood in the large room was morose, to say the least, with clusters of patrons gathered around their meals whispering furiously. I caught snippets of their conversations as I wound between and around their tables headed to an empty spot near a window.

"Poor thing! Maybe she was thrown from the train by the beast!"

"Ridiculous, Sarah! The child is in the bowels of the locomotive, hiding under the coals or something!"

"But they searched my compartment twice. Am I a suspect, do you think?"

I took my seat and a waiter quickly approached to take my luncheon order. I wrote in my notebook: *Is the child already dead?* Sad as that would be, it would explain the silence of the crime, an unexplained clue that stuck in my mind like a burr on a jumper. But why attack a mother and child in such a brutal way? And on a train where you could not make a quick getaway? I took a glance around the room at all the gossiping people and shook my head. I had no evidence of this poor girl's death other than the equally uninformed speculation of my fellow passengers. I ate my meal automatically, barely noting the tartness of the cheese or the warmth of my tea. I took a sip from my cup, looking out the window at the landscape speeding by, thinking about the distraught Mrs. Anderson and her bruised and battered face.

The waiter silently withdrew my empty plate at some point, but I barely noticed, still so deep in thought.

Suddenly I jerked upright: she had known her kidnapper — that was why the girl didn't scream! I sat there for a moment, undecided. Or was it? Was it the explanation? Or was that the explanation I was being led to? I shook my head again. This wasn't a person lying to me: it was the evidence speaking — or the lack of evidence, actually. No one had heard Leah scream or seen her struggle to get away. *Not every book is poisoned, Portia,* I seethed.

I dropped my napkin and made a beeline for Mrs. Anderson's compartment.

CHAPTER FIVE

O utside Mrs. Anderson's compartment were stationed two men, one a junior constable and the other an equally young conductor. They were speaking in low tones when I stopped in front of the door.

They stopped talking abruptly, and the constable said, "May I help you, miss?"

"Yes," I replied, crossing my arms behind my back. "I'd like to speak to Mrs. Anderson, please."

They looked at each other confusedly and then the constable spoke again. "Ah, and are you a friend, Miss...?"

"Adams, and as much as I feel for Mrs. Anderson, we just met today," I answered honestly. "I have to ask her a few more questions that may shed some light on the whereabouts of her daughter."

That got the men's attention, and they both started questioning me at once, so I raised my right hand. "You are welcome to accompany me into the compartment and witness our interaction, gentlemen, but I cannot solve this mystery until you let me through that sliding door."

I waited patiently for them to decide, the conductor looking to the young constable for guidance.

"Really, what harm could I do?" I said. "You can watch me the whole time, and I swear to you I only want to help. My name is Portia Adams, and I live at 221B Baker St. If you are worried, you can contact Scotland Yard and ask for either Chief Inspector Archer or Constable Brian Dawes. Both would vouch for me."

"You work at the Yard?" the conductor asked incredulously.

"I have done business with them, yes," I replied, cognizant of how mysterious that sounded but hoping I wouldn't have to go into detail about the relationship.

The constable's brow furrowed for a moment then he nodded, stepping aside to let me in.

"Thank you," I said, sliding open the door.

Mrs. Anderson sat wanly in the same position as before, leaning slightly to the left in an obviously drugged state, but Mr. Arnold fairly leapt up at seeing us.

"Anything new?" he demanded of me.

"No, I am sorry," I said and then looked at the glassy-eyed woman whose cheek had been bandaged since last I saw her. "Mrs. Anderson, how are you holding up?"

She sniffed, eyes unfocused as the constable followed me into the now full compartment.

"She has been drifting in and out, I'm afraid," Mr. Arnold explained, sitting back down beside her with a sigh.

"I confess I'm surprised to still find you in here, sir," I said, taking a seat opposite. "I expected you to be searching the train with Constable Perkins..."

"And so I would prefer, Miss Adams," he answered, slapping his thigh in obvious frustration, "but I could not leave this poor girl alone. But now that you are here—"

But he did not get the chance to finish his hopeful sentence as Mrs. Anderson sobbed and reached out to hold his hand tightly.

"Please, no, stay with me, Mr. Arnold. I feel safer when you are here," she entreated softly.
Mr. Arnold of course acquiesced.

I gave her a moment to get her emotions under control and then said, "Mrs. Anderson, there is something about this case that has puzzled me. When you were struck down here, why did Leah not scream for help?"

Mrs. Anderson shuddered dramatically and I felt a frisson of unease. Finally, she said, "I don't know! Why do you make me imagine what was being done to my child to prevent her from screaming?"

I felt the eyes of the men in the room turn on me in remonstration, and that frisson ran up my spine again.

"Could it be?" I pressed, pushing down my insecurities about my instincts, "that she knew her kidnapper and therefore was not frightened of him?"

Mrs. Anderson's eyes widened in shock and she shook her head vigorously. "No! No!" she said, tears ready to spill again.

Mr. Arnold reached out to steady her, and the constable asked me, "You think the little girl didn't scream because she knew the kidnapper? Even if she knew who it was, she would have screamed upon seeing her mother hit, would she not?"

I bit my lip because of course she would have — *another mistake, Portia!* It would have been most upsetting to see your mother beaten right in front of you, especially to a young girl. I looked to Mrs. Anderson, who was still shaking her head and mumbling, "No, no! He can't be allowed to get away with that ... not that!"

I focused on that. "He?" I said, leaning forward at the same time as the constable. "Who is 'he', Mrs. Anderson?"

She gulped, blinking quickly. "My husband ... we've been having problems..."
I tilted my head at this new possibility, matching the constable's raised eyebrows.

"But Mrs. Anderson, you told me you were on your way to meet your husband," said Mr. Arnold.

She sniffed before answering. "We are ... we are to meet him in Scotland ... he will be so angry!" She slid slowly to the side, her eyes going unfocused again.

I signaled for the men to step outside with me, but as Mr. Arnold rose to follow, Mrs. Anderson's hand whipped out to grab his arm. She surprised us all with her quick movement, but Mr. Arnold simply grimaced and sank back down to his assigned seat.

As soon as the door slid closed behind us, the constable turned to me excitedly. "I will wire to Edinburgh and have the husband picked up by local authorities. If he is somehow involved in this business we can proceed on that front."

He wasn't looking for my approval, but I nodded anyway and watched him sprint off. I turned thoughtfully back toward my own compartment, analyzing my reaction to Mrs. Anderson's various replies, both oral and physical.

CHAPTER SIX

My experience with James Barclay, a consummate actor who had managed to fool me for most of the investigation involving his father and sister, had left me doubting my own instincts.

I now found myself more paranoid, less likely to believe what I was told and more likely to vacillate between options. My instincts told me that Mrs. Anderson was hiding something. But was that more of the same unfounded paranoia? Why would she lie to me? Her sole mission was to find her daughter, was it not? How could it be anything but? Her fear and worry seemed genuine, but that was just it, they *seemed* genuine. Was she over-dramatizing? What was the normal way to act when one's child was missing, for heaven's sake?

I had been taken in by Barclay's show of concern toward his sister and his poor father. I still got a small shiver of fear when I considered what would have happened if I hadn't mistakenly been poisoned by the books the man was using to murder his father. Would I have followed his clues — sheep-like — and been the first to point my finger at the innocent sister?

I angrily shook my head. Even the great Sherlock Holmes had made mistakes! One of his best-known errors was in underestimating Irene Adler — the woman I now believed to be masquerading as my guardian, under an assumed name.

It would not help to dwell on the mistakes of the past, but it was so hard to move forward without glancing over my shoulder! I had by now been standing outside the door to my compartment for a few minutes. I pressed my head to the glass of the door, trying to make a decision based on fact and not on anxiety. It was hard to make a decision with so few facts. I resolutely lifted my head from the glass — it was time to obtain some facts for myself.

I walked down the long hallway, passing through compartments, nodding at conductors, until I reached the end of the train. Then I turned and walked back, doing my own visual check of the carriages and possible hiding spots. I wasn't subtle in my search, stopping to talk to everyone as I made my way. I came across a couple arguing about the possible hiding spots on a train (their theory was that the child had willfully run away).

Another couple was discussing the possibility that the child had never made it onto the train, that the mother had somehow gotten separated from her daughter on the platform and hit her head and forgotten. I explained why that was unlikely based on the conductor's meeting with the two of them then moved on to the next row of seats in third class.

An elderly woman was asleep in one car and I surprised her when I woke her by moving her six suitcases around to check under and behind them. She threw me out of her compartment, but by and large, people made allowances for my private search.

Halfway back to my seat, I talked to a young mother about the same age as the unfortunate Mrs. Anderson, who half-jokingly offered one of her unruly four to replace Leah. I shook my head as one of these little despots launched a barrage of spitballs in my direction.

I kept moving. It was almost two o'clock. Little Leah had been missing for four hours now, and I was no closer to finding the poor girl.

Another compartment revealed a family of four peacefully reading, happy to allow me to search and very curious about our progress in finding the lost girl. I sadly admitted that, as far as I knew, no progress had been made, and left them to their books.

I kept going, entering compartment after compartment, speaking to passenger after passenger. Some were curious, some were uncaring, and some just wrapped up in their own problems.
One such occupant was a young woman sitting alone in a compartment save for her son, who was sleeping peacefully with his head in her lap.

"He's been very ill," she whispered, large brown eyes worried. I promised to be quick, noting the little boy's sweet face and dark brown hair as he slept unmoving while the mother's eyes watched me conduct my search. I left as quickly as I could. In the next compartment I found a few businessmen who were annoyed with the repeated searches and at first refused me access. I stepped back and offered to find Constable Perkins so that he could ascertain just what it was they had to hide, and was quickly (if grudgingly) given the access I needed to cross their compartment off my list.

By the time I got back to my compartment, it was a quarter past three, and I had to admit that I was no closer to solving this case than before I had started my search.

"At least I saw with my own eyes that Leah is not in the passenger cars of the train," I mumbled, sitting down and pushing off my shoes with a relieved sigh. I closed my eyes for a moment, fighting down the fear that I had missed something obvious, and cursing James Barclay for making me doubt myself.

CHAPTER SEVEN

A knock at the door startled me out of my brief slumber. A glance at my watch told me I'd been asleep for almost an hour, though I felt less rested.

"Come in!" I called, putting my shoes back on and recognizing Constable Perkins through the glass.

Perkins entered, followed by the younger constable who had been present for my interview with Mrs. Anderson. Both men looked tired but removed their hats respectfully as they entered, their body language communicating the state of the search.

"Miss Adams, Borgin here tells me that ye were instrumental in revealing our new lead with Mr. Anderson in Edinburgh," Perkins said.

I looked at them and nodded slowly. "Has he been questioned, then? That was remarkably fast!"

They took a seat on the bench across from me as Perkins answered. "Yes, ma'am. Mr. Anderson was discovered at court. The man is a well-known Crown prosecutor in the area, with many friends in the local police force. He seemed by all accounts surprised and terribly worried about his wee daughter's kidnapping."

I sat back. "Then he is no longer a suspect in having orchestrated the attack in some way?"
"Well, I wouldna say that," Perkins said, glancing at Borgin. "The man is awfully well-connected, though, and has caused quite a stir in Edinburgh. The implication that he might have been responsible for this whole affair sent him tae the highest levels of the police. And from what I hear, he wasna very polite in his pursuit."

"He admitted, though quite angry about our intrusion, that he and his wife have been separated for over a year," Borgin put in.

"This trip, according tae Mr. Anderson," Perkins said, flipping open his notebook to read from it, "was their last-ditch effort to fix their marriage. Sounds tae me like a man who was ready tae be rid of his wife and make a fresh start with his wee girl."

"Then you are holding him in Edinburgh until we arrive, in the hopes that when we get there, his accomplice on board this train will reveal himself to pass the child to the father?" Without waiting for a reply, I continued, "Well, at least in that scenario, we need not worry about the safety of Leah. Her father would of course have paid for her to be well-treated."

"'Holding' him is a strong word," Perkins said with a snort. "The man has demanded tae be kept totally up tae date on any findings, and I am to check in wi' him once an hour by wire."

I scratched my chin. "There is more here. More that has made you suspicious of Mr. Anderson."

Perkins and Borgin looked at each other, confirming my suspicions, but then Perkins cleared his throat and said, "Any other findings we have made, Miss Adams, we daren't share, those being police findings." He clasped and unclasped his hands twice, an obvious tell if I had ever seen one. Finally, when I remained silent, a technique employed and recommended by Holmes in his personal notes on interviewing, Perkins cleared his throat again and spoke. "Miss Adams, you should know that in addition to wiring Edinburgh, we also contacted the London police tae find out more about Mrs. Anderson, Mr. James Arnold ... and yourself."
I nodded. "Of course, under the circumstances that makes complete sense, sir. My curiosity about the case could easily have been due to an involvement in the crime. What did you discover?"

Borgin looked surprised at my casual acceptance of being treated like a suspect, but Perkins, reminding me a bit of Constable Dawes, answered, "Your reputation with Scotland Yard was most positive, young lady, astonishingly so, I would say, unless one kenned your further connections with the offices of Sherlock Holmes."

I tilted my head in admission of these connections. "Then I am no longer a suspect, sir? Because if I am, I would like the opportunity to prove my innocence before we go any further."

Perkins held up his hand. "In addition tae your good name among my peers at the Yard, I can see no motive for ye tae harm Mrs. Anderson or her daughter. You are not a suspect."

"But?" I prodded.

"But, tae be frank, we could use all the help we can get," Perkins admitted. "We have four hours till we arrive at Edinburgh, and while we intend tae bar all exits with our constables, who will look over every passenger and then sweep over the train, but I sturt, t'tell you the truth I do..."

"Because once we've stopped, the opportunity to escape doubles," I finished for him.

"Exactly," he said. "But while we're in motion, while we ken that the bairn and her captor are on board — that is our best opportunity tae get her back."

"Agreed!" I said, standing up decisively. "What can I do to help? I already conducted my own thorough search of the passenger compartments from third class all the way back here. What is next?"

"I want tae explore your theories as tae why little Leah didn't raise a fuss when her mother was hit and she was taken out of her compartment," he replied, flipping through his notebook again. "This idea that she was taken by someone she knew..."

I started pacing a bit in the confined quarters. "I do wish we had some tea to help us think," I said under my breath.

Perkins immediately turned to Borgin and the younger man ran out, presumably to find a waiter to deliver us a pot.

I continued to pace. "If the father hired someone Leah knew to kidnap her, why did Mrs. Anderson not recognize that person?"

"She stated that she saw naught," replied Perkins, reading from his notebook. "She says that the door was slid open, she turned towards the sound and something hard chibbed her across the face."

"Chibbed?" I echoed with a frown, not understanding.

"Ah, struck her across the face," explained Perkins.

"So Mrs. Anderson is hit by someone both she and the child know, but the mother doesn't see them," I mused, pacing still. "Even if I knew the person who had just hit my mother, I confess, it would still make me scream, unless I somehow harbored ill will for my mother. Has there been any evidence of that?"

"Nae, not at all, all reports are that mother and child were extremely close," replied Perkins, watching me pace.

Borgin reappeared, followed by a waiter carrying the requested pot of tea. I thanked them both and poured us all a cup. I sat down to drink mine despite still feeling the urge to pace.

"What if the kidnapper drugged the girl?" offered Borgin, eager to contribute.

"Before or after hitting the mother?" Perkins replied.

"After," Borgin said, and then his face fell. "That would still not account for the silence of the child."

"Well, it might," I said, "if it was a quick enough attack."

We all considered that for a moment until Borgin said, "But even then the kidnapper would have had to carry the unconscious child out into the hallway and all the way down the train to wherever they are right now. Someone would have seen them, wouldn't they? Passengers would have noticed an unconscious child."

One pot of tea gone, we all glumly thought about that as Borgin rang for another pot.

"What if the assailant threatened Leah?" I said, pacing again as I felt the clock ticking against us. "After hitting her mother," I pantomimed the action and then pointed threateningly at Borgin, "he tells Leah that if she screams or fights him, he will kill her mother?"

"The bastirt!" cursed Perkins, considering the horrible scenario. "Apologies, Miss Adams. But it would account for the poor child not making a scene, and still remaining quiet five hours after being kidnapped."

We continued to throw out ideas, each of us managing to rationalize a reason it couldn't be possible and forcing us to keep thinking.

"Could Leah have hit her mother?" Borgin asked hesitantly.

Perkins and I looked at each other and shook our heads at the same time.

"What about one of the conductors? They've been helping with the search. Have any of them been steering the search away from compartments?" I asked, "or rushing you through a section of the train?"

This time Perkins and Borgin shook their heads.

We were halfway through our second pot of tea by now, and a knock at the door drew Borgin out of the conversation again.

"What was discovered about Mr. Arnold?" I asked, determined to leave no rock unturned.

"Nothin'" answered Perkins, running his hand over his bald pate. "He's a businessman, traveling with some partners in a compartment two doors down, and they corroborate his story. Nae connection tae the Andersons, nae criminal background, nae connection tae the husband in Edinburgh, nae debts, nae motive."

Borgin re-entered, looking unhappy, to update us on the search. With difficulty, the search party had made contact with the front engine room, and that too had been ruled out as a potential hiding place for the girl and her captor. I drank another cup of tea as Perkins and Borgin talked, planning a new strategy for the search.

No one on board had seen or heard anything. How was that possible? The searches had been immediate and continuous. Though the luggage car had been searched multiple times, Perkins told Borgin to start opening anything that could fit a small body.

I closed my eyes against that thought, but Borgin dutifully left without argument to pursue his grim assignment. Perkins thanked me for my help, asked me to come find him if I thought of anything else and then followed Borgin out the door.

I sighed, finishing my cup and staring out the window.

CHAPTER EIGHT

Putting aside the fact that the physical searches had been completely fruitless, there was also the problem of the passengers witnessing nothing.

How was the child being hidden so thoroughly and successfully? Her description had been widely transmitted up and down the train, officially and unofficially. A silent crime, a silent victim and a silent perpetrator. I couldn't recall a case from my grandfather's shelves that presented such a list of obstacles.

I decided the least I could do was to sit with Mrs. Anderson. Heading to the dining car, I ordered my third pot of tea (my first three-pot problem — Mr. Holmes would be so proud) to be delivered to her compartment rather than mine. In the casebook titled "The Adventure of the Red-Headed League" my grandfather had described a particularly tense moment wherein Sherlock Holmes had turned to him and referred to the complexity of the case as a 'three-pipe problem'. Holmes measured the difficulty of working through the clues by the amount of time it took for him to smoke three pipes of tobacco. Moving on to my third pot of tea, I silently agreed; this was a complex case indeed when measured through the consumption of our respective drugs.

When I knocked on the door, Mr. Arnold answered, looking restless.

"Oh yes, Miss Adams, do come in, I must stretch my legs," he said, turning toward Mrs. Anderson, who had opened her mouth to protest. "Do not worry, my dear, I am not going on a long search, just to spend some time with my friends in the next compartment. I will knock on the wall as soon as I get there, I promise."

He whispered to me, "She has been most distraught, of course, and has not allowed me out of her sight save for a few minutes, poor thing!"
I thought that a trifle strange and said so in the same low tone.

Mr. Arnold shrugged as we exchanged places. He shut the door as he left.

Mrs. Anderson looked terrible, her face a motley range of colors and her red-rimmed eyes darting everywhere at once. Obviously the sedative had worn off.

"I've asked for a pot of tea to be delivered here," I said, taking the seat across from her.

She nodded, eyes still on the door. In her hands was the small pink jacket her daughter had taken off before this whole nightmare had started for the two of them. She was worrying at it, fidgeting with the buttons, running her fingers over the seams.

A knock sounded from the couch behind where I was sitting, signaling that Mr. Arnold had rejoined his friends. Mrs. Anderson seemed to tense at the knock and then, her shoulders dropping, relaxed when she realized what it meant.

"Mrs. Anderson, I hope you know that the search continues," I said, trying to impart some comfort but unsure what could possibly make her feel better.

She nodded again, and then started when another knock rang out — this time from her closed door. Opening her drapes, I invited the waiter in. He took his time putting down his wares, probably eager to gather some gossip for the dining car. He finally left, and I poured two cups of tea. Mrs. Anderson held hers closely, content, it seemed, to warm her hands against it rather than actually drink it.

I didn't know what else to say to the poor woman, so my eyes strayed around the compartment to the square suitcase on the upper luggage shelf. There was one other suitcase on the shelf, but it was neatly lined up with the front bar of the shelf. This one was askew, almost precarious in its positioning.
Curious, I stood up and carefully tested its weight.

"Don't touch that!" Mrs. Anderson said shrilly.

I jerked my hand back from the luggage in surprise, turning to her with a raised eyebrow.

"It's Leah's," she said in a choked voice.

It wasn't a big case, perhaps two feet by two feet in size, but even my slight test had revealed a surprising heft to it. I wondered how she had carried it in here. And why it didn't go into the luggage compartment, like my own heavy valise?

"A porter must have helped you get it in here," I remarked, sitting back down to my tea. She nodded, hugging the coat and her tea to her chest. That explained the placement of the first suitcase but not the positioning of the second. If the train had caused the luggage to move, would not both of them have moved?

Another knock at the door startled poor Mrs. Anderson to the point that the contents of her teacup slopped all over the small pink coat she had been cradling. As Constable Perkins slid open the door, Mrs. Anderson burst into tears and the poor constable looked very confused, so I did my best to comfort the woman. The stress was obviously unbearable; she was getting worse as time wore on.

Between the two of us, we convinced her to lie down and take a nap. She only agreed when I did as she asked and checked on Mr. Arnold one compartment away. I found the older man deep in conversation with his three mates and returned to give her these assurances. Only then did she slide down in her chair, still clutching the now-wet coat, and close her eyes.

We slid the door closed behind her, and Perkins said, "We are a half hour from the station, Miss Adams, and thirty of my people await us when we get there. We may have failed tae find her, but Leah and her kidnapper still have tae make it past all our officers." I nodded, rubbing wearily at my eyes. Something was still bothering me. "Why is Mrs. Anderson so concerned about Mr. Arnold, do you think?"

He seemed surprised. "I hadn't given it much thought, why? Does it strike ye as strange? Do you think Mrs. Anderson suspects him?"

I rubbed my eyes again. I didn't know what to think, or who to trust. "No, that's not it. Why would she want to keep her assailant close? That makes no sense..." He waited patiently for the reason behind my question, but the truth was, I couldn't articulate it. It was just an unsettled feeling — which I admitted with a frustrated sigh.

He shook his head. "This is a trying case, and right now, I will admit only tae ye, I cannae see how it turns out well for wee Leah." He suggested I head back to my compartment for our arrival, and I, having no other ideas, did as I was told.

I slid open the door to my compartment with an angry swing and slammed it shut with equal emotion. I was missing something – I knew I was!

My leather satchel had slipped to the floor again, so I tossed it back up on the shelf and stalked around the enclosed space, flipping through my notebook. The train had started to slow as I read, and the anger drained out of me, replaced by a leaden sense of failure. I stopped pacing, leaned back against the sliding door and, closing my eyes, tried to focus on that inner voice that was trying to tell me something important. The problem was all the other voices that inserted doubts and fought for control of my decisions.

The train jerked slightly and my satchel slid off the luggage shelf again to land at my feet.

My eyes snapped back open.

That was it!
I grabbed the satchel, threw it over my shoulder and went into the hallway, negotiating my way through first class. Stopping at the door right before Mrs. Anderson's, I knocked and was asked in by the older gentlemen I knew to be within.

"Why, Miss Adams!" remarked Mr. Arnold, extending his hand. "You should sit down, the train is coming to a stop and you could injure yourself!"

I ignored his advice and instead asked, "Sir, when you found Mrs. Anderson unconscious, was her luggage on the floor beside her or up top on the luggage shelf?"

He looked surprised again but answered directly. "Why ... on the floor beside her. I know because I lifted the cursed thing back onto the shelf myself. I at first thought it was that which had hit her!"

"It was!" I answered excitedly as the station came into view. We both exited the compartment and headed toward Mrs. Anderson's compartment, outside of which stood Constable Perkins in discussion with various men.

"Constable Perkins, I hope you have enough men to cover all the exits, because I must ask you for your personal attention immediately," I announced, trying not to sound bossy.

He took in my excited demeanor and his eyes widened. "I dinnae believe it. You've found her?"

"I am close, I think," I said, hesitating and cursing James Barclay again for my lack of confidence. "But I need your help to close this case." I turned to his men. "Please make sure to hold all passengers in their compartments until Constable Perkins tells you otherwise."

They looked to Perkins, who nodded, and then they left in various directions.

I led him and Arnold the rest of the way to Mrs. Anderson's compartment, where I knocked for the last time, just as the train screeched to a halt.

She was sitting bolt upright, staring out the window, and glanced up when I knocked. A look of worry ran across her bruised features as she nodded for us to enter.

"Mrs. Anderson, I have good news!" I announced, entering, followed closely by the constable and Arnold.

"Good news?" she repeated, tensing.

"Yes, I believe we have located Leah!" I said, watching her closely.

"W-what?" she stammered, turning white as a sheet and pressing her hand against her heart.

"Aren't you pleased, Mrs. Anderson?" I asked, directing the constable's attention to the small suitcase I had earlier examined. "We can take you to her, just let us get your luggage for you..."

Mrs. Anderson rose unsteadily as she said "NO!" but Constable Perkins had already wrestled the heavy case down to the floor with a thud.

I made quick work of the straps while Mrs. Anderson stood shaking, and I opened the case.

"What the hell?" whistled Perkins as the lid popped open to reveal several large rocks, a pink dress and a blonde wig.

"Oh, oh no!" whispered Mrs. Anderson, sinking to her knees beside the damning case.

Perkins looked to me for an explanation, so I pointed at Mrs. Anderson's bruised and bandaged face. "There was no assailant, Constable Perkins," I said. "Mrs. Anderson pulled this case onto herself to make it look like she was assaulted. It's why no one heard anything or saw anything. There was nothing to see or hear! There was no assault. There was no kidnapping."

"But ... why?" Perkins said, looking between the case and the sobbing woman as Mr. Arnold stooped to pick up one of the rocks with two hands and stare at it incredulously.

"Because she is about to divorce her husband," I said with a rueful shake of my head. "And I expect she feared losing custody of their daughter. Or maybe she just wanted to cause her soon-to-be-ex-husband a measure of pain?"

I asked the last in a harsher tone, not expecting an answer, but I received one, much to my surprise:

"He deserves some pain — the bastard," she hissed up at me.

I crouched. "Why go through so much trouble to hide your daughter from your husband?"

She sniffed once, twice. "Alan ... he ... he beats me," she whispered. I recoiled, but she continued. "It started when we were first wed, and it's gotten steadily worse as time went on."

She sniffed again, looking down. "When I had Leah, I had hoped it would stop — but it didn't." Another sniff, a gulp. "It got worse! And then last year, at Christmas ... he hit Leah! So hard that she fell down the stairs."

I glanced up at Perkins, whose face reflected my shock. Mr. Arnold had dropped the rock and now covered his eyes with his hand.

"That was when I left him," she snarled, defiantly meeting my eyes.

"Why are you here then at all, ma'am?" asked Perkins gently, crouching down beside me.

"Not by choice!" she fairly spat. "His lawyer friends drew up papers that required me to bring Leah, and the police, when I went to them, told me there was naught they could do! That was when I knew I had to do something to protect my daughter from him — permanently!"

I rocked back on my heels, turning toward Perkins with a question in my eyes. He anticipated it and answered, "My background check into Mr. and Mrs. Anderson did reveal numerous unexplained trips to the hospital and at least two occasions when police were called to the residence by concerned neighbors."

"We live in a townhouse," she explained, eyes wet. "They could hear my cries. But when the police arrived, every time, and it was far more than twice, my husband convinced them that I had somehow injured myself."

Perkins shook his head. "He wouldnae have fooled me!"

"Or me!" announced Arnold angrily.

I believed her story, God help me, even after the fiasco with the Barclays. Even with the secrets my guardian kept from me. This woman was not acting, and she felt true fear for her child, that was clear in her story and in the corroborating evidence. But what could be done? Even now the man was probably standing feet away on the platform outside!

Perkins again anticipated my thoughts. "Where is Leah?"

When she stayed stubbornly silent, I replied for her, "Safe," said I, snapping the suitcase closed again, "and if we three say nothing, will remain that way."

Mrs. Anderson gasped at my words, but Mr. Arnold was already nodding vigorously.

With my arm around her, I said to Perkins, "These are your choices as I see them, sir. Either you arrest this woman for making a false allegation and hand a poor defenseless child over to a known abuser. Or we erase the events of the last few minutes and continue as if we still don't know Leah's whereabouts."

Mr. Arnold moved around to stand on the other side of Mrs. Anderson, indicating his opinion on the subject. This left Constable Perkins stonily looking at the three of us, and I will admit I did not envy him his choice. I had been advised and had experienced this middle ground of justice before. I knew my decision to be one I could live with, but perhaps Perkins, with a lifetime of defending the law, could not.

A knock at the door startled us all out of our stand-off, and Constable Borgin slid open the door.

"Sir, Crown Prosecutor Anderson is demanding to see his wife," explained the younger constable. Perkins' back was still to the door, with the three of us — Arnold, Anderson and myself — facing it, so only we saw the senior constable grit his teeth.

"You can escort Mrs. Anderson t'see Crown Prosecutor Anderson, but I want you tae stay with them the whole time," he said finally.

I squeezed her shoulder, still unsure of what Perkins was going to do, and she turned fearfully toward me. Then I gave her a hug, whispering in her ear as I did so. "Say nothing, stick to your story. If it all comes out, it all comes out, and it will do no more harm than has already been done."

She wilted in my arms at my words and I had to help her to the door and pass her on to Constable Borgin. The door slid closed behind them as I opened my mouth to ask after Perkins' intentions, but he spoke first. "I want tae know where Leah is, an' I want tae know how ye discovered her, Miss Adams, and I want tae know now."

I looked at Mr. Arnold, who just pursed his lips, and I realized it was up to me.

"The truth is that all I have is theory, but I believe it to be a good one," I hedged, "and it starts with Mr. Arnold."

"I have a feelin' your theories are uncommonly correct, Miss Adams. Tell us on the way tae Leah," said Perkins, opening the door and ushering me out into the hallway.

"Once I realized that Mrs. Anderson had inflicted those wounds upon herself, I was left with some answers to some key questions," I said, leading the way. "Leah didn't scream, because her mother was never beaten, that much was clear. So when did Leah disappear? Well, obviously not after her mother knocked herself unconscious. Somehow Leah was not in the compartment. Sometime between meeting Mr. Arnold and Mr. Arnold discovering Mrs. Anderson on the floor, Leah left the compartment."

"I follow ye, but how? By herself?" answered Perkins, right at my heels.

"By no means. She was walked from her mother's compartment to where she is right now by Mrs. Anderson's accomplice," I said, weaving around two conductors. "I think I may have even seen her being led in this direction when I was in my compartment. But the key is who saw her and who did not. It is why Mr. Arnold was never permitted to join the search. He was the only one on the train, other than Mrs. Anderson, who knew what Leah looked like."

Perkins interrupted. "We all had a description!"

"You had the wrong description — as evidenced by the dress and wig we found in the luggage, sir," I corrected. "And I am betting even the birthmark was fabricated by Mrs. Anderson in order to further confuse our searches."

"But then I was working under the same conditions as any of you," said Mr. Arnold from the back of our little group. "I too knew Leah to be a blonde child in a pink dress with a red birthmark. If that was all for show, I would have been hard-pressed to recognize her!"

By now we had arrived at our destination in third class. I stopped, slightly out of breath, and turned toward Mr. Arnold and Constable Perkins. "Well, let's test that theory, shall we, gentlemen?" I slid open the compartment.

Inside sat a woman I had interviewed a few hours earlier, in the exact same position as before, with her son's sleeping head resting on her lap.

Mr. Arnold entered the compartment, glancing around, at first not understanding. Then finally he gasped when he took a good look at the child. The woman, realizing she had been found out, tensed, her hands balling into fists.

"This ... this is Leah Anderson," Arnold managed to stammer, pointing at the child in the woman's arms. "Her hair is dark and short, and the poor thing is dressed like a small boy, but it is her, I would swear to it, Constable."

"We searched this compartment twice," Perkins said incredulously, "but we were looking for a blonde girl with a birthmark ... not a sickly boy with dark hair."

"Exactly," I said, taking a moment to look out at the platform to see a huge man in a tailored suit yelling at the crowd around him. *That must be Mr. Anderson,* I thought, shaking my head as Mrs. Anderson was escorted to his side. She was a brave woman; despite the fact that he dwarfed her by a stone and a foot, she still allowed herself to be placed in front of his terrifying ire.
"How did she get here?" Perkins demanded from the woman seated in front of us.

The woman looked down at the sleeping child then back up at the constable.

"We know everything, ma'am," I counseled gently. "We found the wig and the dress. Even now, Mrs. Anderson is outside with her husband."

The woman closed her eyes briefly, and then opened them. "I met Mrs. Anderson in first class as we arranged ... we took off Leah's wig and dressed her like a boy. We told her it was a game," she explained haltingly. "Then Leah and I ran back and jumped on the train in third class with tickets I had purchased beforehand."

"Why is she still sleeping?" I asked, putting my hand on the girl's forehead.

"Opium in her milk," she answered, eyes on Perkins. "We felt it was more plausible that the child be explained as sick rather than try to keep her quiet."

Perkins ran his hand over his bald head. "What is your name, ma'am? How are you connected to all 'o this?"

"Mrs. Layton is my name," she said, stroking the child's head. "I am a friend of Mrs. Anderson's mother, and I am helping them to ensure that that man out there never strikes this sweet baby ever again." At her words, I looked at Perkins for his reaction. He was a good man and flinched a bit.

"You cannot send the child back to that man, Constable!" said Arnold, shaking his head.

"Please, you must help us!" begged Mrs. Layton. "Nothing can be done to save Mrs. Anderson, poor girl, but we can still save her daughter ... please!"
"There are ways to do this, Constable, please," I said, adding my voice to their entreaties, wishing Constable Brian Dawes was here to help me and wondering at the same time if he would agree with my interpretation of the law.

But Perkins hung his head before saying, "My conscience aside, I cannae willfully lie tae this father. This is a crime. This whole endeavor has been criminal, and I cannae condone it, no matter how justified it is."

He turned toward the door, no longer able to face us. "I go now t'speak to the man. Ye should follow the crowd and speak to the constable at your door. I believe it is Tooms. He will escort you to us."

So saying, he walked out of the compartment, shoulders hunched.

Mrs. Layton tenderly kissed the top of Leah's short-cropped head, and then we helped her stand, draping the child over her so that her head rested comfortably against the woman's shoulder. Mr. Arnold sadly placed the boy's cap over the sleeping child's head, and I led them out of the compartment into the stream of people being shepherded off the train.

I wracked my brain for an escape route, but there was none to be found. Besides, Perkins knew the truth now and would be honor-bound to pursue Mrs. Layton and myself if we by some miracle did make it away from here. As we neared the steps to the platform where a constable stood checking passengers, I could hear Mr. Anderson threatening violence to any and all a few yards away. From my raised vantage point, I could see the large man berating Constable Borgin and shaking Mrs. Anderson by the arm as he yelled.

She wasn't even struggling despite the pain he was obviously causing her, but Constable Perkins finally got to her side and managed to pry the man's hand off her arm, pulling her behind him to speak to Mr. Anderson directly. Mr. Anderson could have played American football — that was how big he was, with huge, meaty hands and massive shoulders. The man had to be at least two hundred pounds, and his face and neck were crimson with anger. He was sweating from the exertion of yelling and waving his arms around; his baldpate and the dark hair over his ears sheened with it.

Whatever Perkins said to Anderson obviously incensed him more, because the man actually shoved the constable backward, to the surprise of the policemen gathered all around. A few more minutes of negotiating did nothing to lower the man's temper, and it didn't even seem he was listening to Perkins, just railing on about the stupidity of the entire force and the weakness of his useless wife. He bellowed that when he found his daughter he would never allow her out of his sight again, and never allow his wife to be trusted with her alone again, and pointed a meaty finger at the woman even as she stood behind Constable Perkins. Her head was lowered, poor thing, well used to this level of abuse, I was sure.

I gritted my teeth, wondering how I could hand this poor child into the hands of such a man, when Perkins turned away from the terrifying man, made eye contact with me, and nodded once.

I didn't even hesitate. I put my arm around Mrs. Layton and said to the constable in front of me, "Constable Tooms, we need to get Billy to a doctor right away, he's been ill for the whole trip. Can you help us, please? Constable Perkins told me you would see to our hasty departure."

The young constable wavered, looked to his superior, who nodded once more, and then we were escorted out of the fray, off the platform, and to freedom.

CHAPTER NINE

B ut then what will happen to Mrs. Anderson?" demanded my guardian as she lit the wood in the enormous fireplace.

"I suppose she must suffer until the investigation ends and she gets her divorce, poor woman," I said, shaking my head at the prospect. "But Constable Perkins knows all now. He will keep a close eye on her through his peers in her local precinct, I am hopeful. I have arranged a luncheon with him tomorrow to talk about the case. He is most troubled but sure he made the right decision, good man."

The fireplace crackled invitingly, and the beautiful decorations sparkled all round us in this great hall. Once I had delivered Mrs. Layton and her precious package to the nearest horse-drawn hackney, I had returned to the platform, where my guardian awaited me, watching Mr. Anderson's tirade. I hesitated for a moment, remembering my real purpose here, and was glad to see her attention was directed at Anderson rather than me.

She had shaken her head at his diatribe, and together we retrieved my valise and left the place as quickly as possible.

This grand home was just outside Edinburgh near East Lothian, though it was "on loan from my good friend Major William Baird," my guardian had explained, without really explaining, as usual.

"And you didn't feel even once that the perpetrator of this case deserved to be brought to justice?" Mrs. Jones asked curiously from her cushioned chair under a thick wool blanket.

I heard a car engine outside the house, listening to it slow and then pass before shaking my head steadfastly. "Mrs. Anderson has been punished enough and — as she says — her husband not enough."
"And the ghost of Mr. James Barclay?" she asked knowingly, reaching for her tiny clay pipe.

"Just that," I replied, leaning back in my chair with a determined grimace. "A ghost. Ephemeral. Invisible. Immaterial. And not something that can stand between me and the truth."

That word sat in the air between us for a few beats, and then we both spoke at the same time.

"Portia, I must—"

"Mrs. Jones, it's time—"

We smiled at each other nervously, and then I raised my hand in invitation for her to continue.

"I must admit that I brought you here under ... somewhat false pretenses," she said, taking a steadying pull from her pipe.

I frowned. "I don't understand, ma'am." And then my eyes flew wide at a thought. "Do not tell me that we are not actually in the home of a friend! Oh, please don't tell me that we are ... I don't know ... squatting in some rich family's home without their permission?"

A deep laugh from somewhere behind us caused me to twist around in my chair, knocking throw pillows to the floor, as a tall man stepped from the darkness to say, "Our granddaughter knows you well, Madam Adler, despite your machinations to hide your identity from her."

"Your ... your what?" I whispered, now standing on shaking legs as the man approached us, resisting the urge to back up only because my curiosity was slightly greater than my shock. But only slightly.

"Granddaughter," said the lean man, finally stepping far enough into the firelight for me to recognize cold gray eyes over a thin hawk-like nose.

He was approximately the same height as I, and though fifty years my senior, had the posture and bearing of a man much younger. His hair was iron-gray, receding in the front, emphasizing the widow's peak I had seen in photos. His square chin, though, was the one physical feature that made my lower lip tremble. I knew that chin. It was my father's.

"Charles Eagle was my father." I looked to my guardian, who had tears in her eyes but met my gaze with acceptance. "Adler is the German word for Eagle. You changed your name when you had him; when you had my father. That's why my mother left me in your care. You are my grandmother!"

She glanced down for a moment, and then back up, one tear tracking down the wrinkles on her pale face. "Yes, Portia, I wanted my son to have something of my name. Something of me without labeling him as the son of a known criminal."

"And you," I said, turning back to this man who had upended my world, "you and she..."

He didn't even glance toward my guardian, but his eyes narrowed, and I saw her flinch out of the corner of my eye. "Where were you?" I demanded of them. "I was told my father was an orphan! That he had no family!"

"Told by your mother, Portia," Irene Adler said softly, calling my attention back to her, "who married my son after I had to leave the country, and then lost him in a war a few scant months later. Her sorrow was profound. To the point that she cut off all relations with me, blaming me for leaving, blaming me for ... for Charles's death.

"I blamed myself too," Adler continued, taking another shaky draw on her pipe. "I had to leave the country before they were married. I was being pursued by some investigators and was unable to return to the States for years. Your grandmother Constance died as well while I was abroad, so I had no way to gain access to you, no sympathetic ear.

"I sent money and letters, and at first she returned both unopened," she said. "But eventually, as I pushed money on her for your education, she gave in. But she never wrote back to me or asked me back into your lives. I even showed up at your door one day, though you would not remember, you were so small."

Her eyes glistened as she reminisced. "Your mother threw me out and threatened to call the police on me should I ever return."

"And yet, when she died, she left me in your care," I said, wondering at my mother's decision. It must have been so hard on her. Even more so now that I knew just how angry she had been.

"I was the only living relative she knew of," she said, dabbing at her eyes, before looking at her former lover. "The only one she trusted."

He didn't respond, choosing to keep his gaze on me.

She stood up to come to my side. "I love you. Surely you know that. Surely even without this revelation, you know that I love you? That I am so happy to have you in my life?"

I tilted my head, trying to be angry with her, but instead just feeling weak with emotion.

I thought of the monogrammed handkerchief she had handed me on our first meeting — IAH — Irene Adler Holmes — and looked at the man who purported to be my grandfather.

"For my part I must admit I refused to believe that our brief union had produced an heir," he said, folding his hands behind his back. "I allowed Madam Adler's denials to push me away despite the evidence in front of my eyes. She had remarried by the time Charles was born, and, I believe, specifically chose her mate based on his physical similarities to me."

I glanced at Adler and found weary admission in the way she waved for him to continue, turning her back on him to warm her hands in front of the fire.

"She divorced him, of course, and remarried at least twice more, moving around the world, doing her best to keep him from my sight. Only when he was ... only when Charles died did I finally accept the truth. And only then with Watson dragging me to the hospice to see him."

His guilt and sadness were writ large on his lined face. For the first time since stepping from the shadows he lowered his gaze from mine. "I cannot ask his forgiveness, and your mother refused to give it. I respected your mother's wishes and never approached she or you in her lifetime."

He hesitated, and then raised his sharp gray eyes to meet mine again. "Now, it is all up to you. Do you want me in your life, or will you, like your mother before you, choose to deny our relationship?"

"This is surreal," I whispered, reaching down to steady myself by putting a hand on the back of the chair I had just vacated, feeling its texture and trying to focus my thoughts. I looked again at the hawk-nosed man. "I was looking for you. I have been trying so hard to connect with my grandfather — with the life he had with you..."

"I know my dear, I know," he answered, the beginnings of a smile starting on his lips. "I have followed your exploits and am thrilled with your work. You have a remarkable mind, and combining that with all the grace and social skills that were so admired in Watson, there is truly nothing you cannot do.

London needs a new consulting detective, and who better than the granddaughter of Holmes and Watson?"

Adler sniffed, her tone confident again as she spoke without turning. "Her mind is her own. Her skills her own. What she chooses to do with them must be her choice as well. Perhaps she will choose a safer course, Sherlock — surely it is what her mother would have wanted. The apartment at Baker Street could just as easily become a law office."

I swallowed painfully, unable to keep the tears from running down my cheeks at the reminder of all my mother had kept from me. "All I wanted was for you to fill in the gaps about Dr. Watson and Constance Adams," I found myself mumbling. "All I wanted was for you to confirm my findings about her — about Irene Adler. And now..."

"And now, my girl, you have found me," Sherlock Holmes said with a sparkle in his eyes I was hesitant to call emotion only because of all I had read about him. He stepped forward to take both my hands in his, the long fingers reminding me of my own. "And imagine how much more we can be — together."

- Fin -

ABOUT THE AUTHOR

Angela Misri is an award-winning journalist, author and instructor living in Toronto. In addition to the Portia Adams series, Misri also writes the *Pickles VS the Zombies* series for children.

AngelaMisri.com

@karmicangel on Twitter & Instagram

9 798669 453510